Sourwood Tales

BOOKS BY *Billy C. Clark*

USELESS DOG

RIVERBOY

THE MOONEYED HOUND

THE TRAIL OF THE HUNTER'S HORN

SONG OF THE RIVER

A LONG ROW TO HOE

GOODBYE KATE

THE CHAMPION OF SOURWOOD MOUNTAIN

SOURWOOD TALES

Sourwood Tales

STORIES BY BILLY C. CLARK

Illustrated by Harold Eldridge

G. P. Putnam's Sons, NEW YORK

Nine of the tales in this volume are published for the first time. The others were previously published as follows: "The Illiterate Spider" in *Boys' Life,* 1967; "Froggie Goes A-Courtin'" in *Boys' Life,* 1960; *Senior Citizens* (as one of best twelve short stories of 1960); *Searchlight* magazine (for the blind), 1960; Scott-Foresman's *American Literature* (college edition), 1967; "Lucy Caught the Moon" in *Trail of the Hunter's Horn,* G. P. Putnam's Sons, 1957; "The Mooneyed Hound," G. P. Putnam's Sons, 1958; as a *Crowell-Collier Classic,* 1960; *Dogs* (an anthology), Platt & Munk, 1962; "The Heart of a Woodsman" in *Boys' Life,* 1960; and in *Searchlight* magazine, 1961; "The Fiddle and the Fruit Jar" in *Coronet* magazine, 1961; "Fur in the Hickory" by University of Kentucky, 1953; "Ely's Bass" in *Boys' Life,* 1962; "Of Greed and Eb Ringtom" in *The Champion of Sourwood Mountain,* G. P. Putnam's Sons, 1966.

Library of Congress Catalog Card Number: 68-15044

PRINTED IN THE UNITED STATES OF AMERICA

To my daughter MELISSA BETH CLARK
and
to my son BILLY C. CLARK, JR.

Contents

Sourwood Tales

1.

The Illiterate Spider

HE was a black and yellow spider and he had spun one end of his web onto a corner of the chicken house roof and the other end onto a sunflower stalk nearby. It was July and the sunflower was in bloom and on my way to feed the chickens I had stopped to stare at the bloom of the sunflower and I saw the spider there. He was near the roof, up where the web whirled into a silver cone and disappeared under the eaves. I thought that inside the cone must be his home. And the great web that poured out to touch the sunflower was that portion of the world that the spider had spun off for himself. I hoped so since it was a portion of the world that I would have no trouble at all staying away from.

The morning was early and the dew silvered the tiny strands of the web and the web danced in the wind as silent as the end of a yawn. And, looking up through the huge web, I could see the broader strands of white, broken and zigzagged and knitted across the web like lightning that had fallen to earth, netted and held timeless.

"You are a pretty spider," I said, "but I am afraid of you."

I heard a noise behind me, turned, and saw my brother Raphrael, thumbs hooked in his belt staring up at the spider with a frown on his face.

"Uh oh!" he said.

And, hoping that Raphrael hadn't been there long enough to have heard me say to the spider that I was afraid of him I said:

"What do you mean uh oh? It's just a spider."

"Nope," Raphrael said. "That's where you're wrong as usual. It's not *just* a spider."

"How come it ain't?" I asked, knowing that Raphrael was smarter than me since he was older and going to school and that was enough to make it so. But I also knew that Raphrael was bad to tease.

"Because he's a *writing spider*," Raphrael said.

"What's that mean?" I asked, swallowed, and tried to squint a quick look at the spider without Raphrael seeing.

"First off it means that I'd be mighty careful if I was you," Raphrael said. "A writing spider is an omen spider. Evil as a witch. Why, if he hears someone's name he just writes it across his web and they shrivel up and die before the sun goes down. I'd be careful if I was you."

I fingered the pan of corn I held in my hand and said:

"Shucks. How do you know something like that?"

"Lots of ways," Raphrael said. "I'm older than you for one thing." And Raphrael had swelled his chest out and was looking independent, chewing on a leaf of Life Everlasting Weed which Ma would have whipped him for doing if she knew it because Ma claimed that the weed was akin to tobacco and that made chewing it wrong. But Raphrael was always doing it and the times he got away with it sure did make him look all grownupitish and important and smart. "For another thing," he said, "Ma told me about that spider once. And, you know something else about that spider?"

"What's that?" I asked, not sure that I wanted to know but too curious not to ask just like I was always doing on things of this sort. I mean like the times when the night was over the mountain and Raphrael would ask me if I would like to see a ghost and I'd say yes not really wanting to and he'd point one out to me and I'd always see it and then Raphrael would threaten to tell Ma on me for trying to sneak the cover from him so that I could hide up to nothing that a ghost could see and leave Raphrael exposed and naked on the bed.

Raphrael squinted his eyes and looked toward the spider. He pointed.

"See them big zigzag threads that look like bolts of lightning?" he asked.

I swallowed again and stared toward the web. And the dew now, touched by a coming sun, scooted across the web, swelled into tears, and dropped toward the

earth popping on the leaves and underbrush below.
I said, slowly:

"I see them."

"Well," Raphrael said, "each one of them threads
is all that is left of some poor fellow. Sure ain't much,
is it!"

"Good gosh!" I said. "Where are they now?"

Raphrael looked all downcast and sad.

"Just shriveled up and gone to dust," he said. "All
snuffed out by a writing spider."

"He don't eat people, does he?" I asked, and hoped
not.

"Seldom, I reckon," Raphrael said. "Eats flies mostly. I guess some of them patches are the names of
flies."

"Shucks," I said. "I never heard of a fly having a
name before."

Raphrael looked as disgusted as he could, frowned,
squirted out some Life Everlasting juice and said:

"Lot's of things you ain't ever heard of before.
You ain't been nowhere and done nothing and it's
a big world. You just ask Ma about the writing spider
if you don't believe me."

Well, I was thinking that Raphrael hadn't been any
farther away than Sourwood School and that was just
to the end of the hollow and four miles away. But
Raphrael being in school and all I couldn't be sure,
and so I thought I had better ask Ma about the writing
spider.

I asked Ma while she was washing clothes. She
looked at me, brushed her hair from her face, and

said that talk of writing spiders wouldn't get much washing done but the answer was yes. She knew that the writing spider was out by the chicken house and that it had been believed forever here in the hill country that if the spider heard your name he would write it across his web and you would die before the sun went down. I asked Ma if *she* believed it, and she swatted some suds from her nose that had splashed up from the tub and said that life was hard enough here in the hill country without going around doubting omens, beliefs and the sorts.

And so of the mornings now I began to take a look at that spider. From where I hoped he couldn't see me, taking a chance since I didn't know anything at all about the eyes of the spider. I mean peeking through brush, looking around corners and such, I watched the wind play with his great web whipping it back and forth like a piece of white lace Ma had hung out to dry on a line. And it was the cleanness of the web that worried me; never a fly in it. Maybe, I thought, Raphrael don't know everything when it comes to a writing spider. Why, maybe the spider didn't eat people at all. But while I stared at the web and thought, goose pimples popped out all over me. A spider had to eat *something*.

My thoughts took a turn for the worse. Maybe this was no ordinary spider that would settle for a little old fly when there was something bigger like me coming his way every day to feed the chickens. I began to see the spider sitting there grinning, honing his ears —if a spider has ears—and being willing to go hungry and wait . . . wait for Raphrael to hand me over, serve me up.

I was certain that Raphrael was set on doing just that. Because every morning now when I stepped inside the chicken house Raphrael would squint through the cracks in the boards and say:

"Who's in there! Are you a fox after Ma's chickens?"

And I'd whisper back through the cracks, "It's only me," sure that Raphrael knew my voice.

I could see Raphrael standing out there with his hands on his hips just like Ma always stood whenever she was uncertain but set to get the truth of something.

"Maybe. And then maybe it ain't," Raphrael said, much louder than I thought he ought with the spider being so close and all. "If it is who you are, then what's your name?"

"Shucks," I'd whisper back, squinting through the cracks to see if Raphrael might be exciting the spider, "you know my name. I'm your brother!"

And with part of one eye and a part of his face showing through the cracks Raphrael would say:

"Oh, then it's you . . ."

I never gave Raphrael time to finish. I dropped the corn from the pan, something that Ma was forever cautioning me never to do since the corn fell in a doodle this way and all the chickens could not get to eat. And when I ran past Raphrael, he laughed hee, hee, hee, hee.

Life just wasn't worth much with a spider at the end of it. I tried to think of ways to change it. Like sneaking up and tearing down the spider's web. But **Raph-**rael took care of that. He said that it was just as much doom to destroy the spider or his belongings. You'd shrivel just the same and maybe even a little worse. Well, I thought of not going to feed the chickens. But this would mean shunning my chore and facing Ma and that was equal any day to facing up to a spider.

Then I thought about just going to Ma and telling on Raphrael. But Raphrael had promised to give me his barlow knife with the handles off whenever I stopped being a tattletale about everything I saw or heard. And if I got Raphrael a whipping, he was sure not to give me the knife, and life probably wouldn't be worth living without it. I was just miserable.

And then one morning while I was spreading the feed out for the chickens and watching the cracks in the boards and thinking that the spider could be getting tired of waiting on Raphrael and might just crawl through a knothole and snatch me, I heard Raphrael say:

"Is it a fox in there this morning or is it only my brother . . . "

And with the visions of the spider in my head I forgot all about the barlow knife. I threw the feed pan into the air, opened the door of the chicken house and yelled:

"Doggone you, Raphrael! I'm going to tell Ma on you right now!"

I heard Raphrael scream *yeeoweeo* and when I stepped out of the chicken house he was sitting on the ground as solemn as a stump.

"What's the matter?" I asked.

"You've just snuffed out your brother!" Raphrael said. "That's what's up. You've told the spider my name."

And I looked toward the great web fairly expecting to see the spider writing poor Raphrael's name across it. I didn't see the spider. Maybe he had gone down into the whirling darkness of the cone to get whatever he needed to write with.

"Gee, Raphrael," I said, "I didn't mean to. It slipped out."

Raphrael jumped to his feet, took a look toward the web and shouted:

"Yeeowee! If he missed my name the first time, he got it for sure the second! I'm probably snuffed out twice!"

And Raphrael ran up the path holding his throat. Maybe from pain. I don't know.

I moped around the rest of the day thinking what an awful thing I had done: telling the spider Raphrael's name not once but twice. Snuffing him out two times in one day.

In the evening Raphrael walked up to me, stoop-shouldered, handed me the knife and said, "I want you to have the knife, Ben." He squinted off toward the top of Sourwood Mountain and there wasn't enought distance between the sun and the top of that mountain to stick a finger through.

"Gee, Raphrael," I said. "I'm sorry." I fondled the knife in my hand.

"It's done," Raphrael said. "Just look after things." He squinted at me.

I squinted longer at Raphrael. Looked for changes that ought to be taking place on someone no farther from shriveling up than the sun was from the top of the mountain.

But the sun went down and nothing happened. In the gathering dusk I found Raphrael sitting around the side of the house and I said:

"What do you think, Raphrael?"

Raphrael coughed and there was a wheeze and a choke on the end of it. His voice quivered.

"I'm tightening up like a worm on a hot rock. It won't be long now. Sure ain't no fun. I mean being snuffed out by a writing spider. And two times makes it twice as worse."

Night came and Ma made us go to bed. I could hear Raphrael breathing hard something awful. I sneaked my toe up against his skin, afraid and expecting to feel the wrinkled hide that I thought ought to be coming to someone as close to shriveling up as Raphrael. But Raphrael's skin felt as slick as a river eel, and he rolled and tossed and took up most of the bed like always.

"What do you think now, Raphrael?" I whispered.

"I'll be gone by morning," he whispered back, low enough for Ma not to hear and scold since she believed that a bed was to sleep in and not to whisper in. "I'm awful weak. Look after Ma and the knife."

And then I heard Raphrael snoring and got sleepy myself and thought I'd just drop off to sleep and snore some myself since Raphrael said I always snored when I slept but said he never did.

I woke early, afraid that Raphrael was nothing

but a corpse beside me. I scooted a toe against him
and he felt warm as a breakfast fire. And then I
saw him pop one eye open and look slowly around.
He felt his face and then the rest of his body. It
all made me happy enough to bust. I said:

"What do you think now, Raphrael?"

Raphrael scratched his head, blinked at me and
said:

"That doggone spider is illiterate!"

"What's that mean, Raphrael?" I asked, not knowing what illiterate meant but figuring and hoping it
was on our side.

"It means he ain't smart enought to know how
to write," Raphrael said.

"Gee, Raphrael," I said, "I sure am glad." I reached
under my pillow and pulled out the barlow knife.
"Does it mean I have to give the knife back?"

But Raphrael was too busy now to answer. He
was going over his hide inch by inch pinching it in
places hard enought to raise a welt. But finally he
said:

"I guess so."

And then Raphrael slid both legs off the edge of
the bed, bounced a few times to test and then stood
up.

"Yep. He's illiterate all right," he said.

"Gosh, Raphrael," I said, "you sure are smart."

Raphrael reached for his britches.

"I know it," he said.

2.
Gift of the Rivers

IT was an old two-story river shack that had been whipped by the floods of the valley for many years. It stood overlooking the junction of the Big Sandy River and the mightier Ohio. And it leaned like an old man bowed by time, peering at the two rivers as if trying to judge their moods. For it had been the rivers that had crooked it, warping its boards until the winds picked at them and made weird noises like the sounds of a harp through the cracks. During the summers small trees sprouted along the roof, their seed brought by the winds and deposited in the rich river muck that the rivers had left in the rotted gutters.

Most of the people of the town had come at least once to stand and stare at the old house, sure that the wind that came up from the rivers would topple it before they had a chance to see it again. And often boys gathered around the house daring each other to stand under the leaning side. Few of them did, but the ones that took the dare left heroes. To all of them it was just

an old river shack ready to fall, but to my older brother John, my little brother Arlie and me, it was home.
And when the rivers were low and calm we played
around it as if it were an old friend, knowing it would
not hurt us. In time of flood we huddled on its second
floor and leaned with it to judge the mood of the two
rivers, willing to live for a portion of time at a seafar-
ing gate in exchange for the cheapness of the rent that
Pa had to pay, and for the privilege of remaining together, the old house and the two rivers included.

Since our way of life depended on what the rivers
would or would not do, it was only natural that our
first schooling should have been of the two rivers. Pa
taught us of the rivers when they were full and angry
in mood. He taught us to read the currents, the quick
rise and fall of the water, the color of the sky; especially when it spoke of rain. Rain had much to do with the
rivers; rain was a part of them.

To misjudge the rivers meant useless moving, sham-
ing us into joining the long processions of townspeople
who knew nothing of the rivers, carrying our household plunder on the backs to the foot of the hills. And
unlike many of the more prosperous people of the
town, we had nowhere to go once we reached the foot
of the hills. There were no homes of friends to shelter us
or our meager belongings; our friends were the river
people living in the river shacks, and they were in the
same position as we were. To us there was only the
side of the lonesome hill with the sky overhead for a
roof. Pa preferred to remain in the two-story shack
with the rivers tucked around us and only take to the

foothills as a last resort. February and March were the flood months here in the mountains, a time of cold winter rains; almost more than one could bear along the foot of the hills without shelter. Pa never spoke-angrily of the rivers, not even as we huddled on the second floor of the shack, feeling the tremble and sway of the wood. Rivers were akin to people in that they had periods of angry moods; it was wrong to judge the character of either at such a time. He even sided with the rivers when it came to the old house. Yes, the rivers would one day claim the house, break it apart and cover the pieces one by one with mud until finally it decayed. But the house was a river shack and this was its fate. A more honorable fate than to go by fire or at the hands of wreckers.

Of the summers Pa opened his small secondhand store that he operated on the first floor of the house. He was busy and Ma took over much of our schooling of the rivers. For Ma loved the rivers too. She told us that to take the green leaves of the cotton willow, pull down a portion of the blue sky, stir them to the right mixture, would be to blend the beautiful color of the summer water. And along the shores we went with her to gather the wild greens that flourished in the rich loam. We cleared away wood drifts to make space for our small garden, and John and I kept a short trotline in the rivers to take fish that we would eat or sell on the streets of town. And of the evening when we went to the rivers to sit and listen to the wind and watch for paddle wheels, we took little Arlie with us and let him climb the backs of the old willows, laughing at him when he straddled them and pretended to be riding a spirited horse. Then John and I would climb up into the tree house we had built and fuss at little Arlie for trying to climb after us because the tree house was too high for him. But as little as he was, he always won, fussing and quarreling louder than the small creek that emptied into the rivers close to the old shack. And then we kept an eye out up the bank for Ma who would whip us good if she knew little Arlie was in the tree house.

But it was the flood months that we liked most on the rivers. For it was then that the rivers brought us gifts.

We huddled now on the second floor of the old house, looking down over the swollen and muddy surface of the rivers. And the rains came and both rivers rose, and from the window we watched a world change before our eyes.

Now in the swift currents of the rivers came houses that had been torn from their footings farther upstream. And the rivers, now like a great ribbon blown by the wind, pulled at the houses until at times only their roofs showed. Chickens, dogs, even cows and horses held to the flat roofs, or straddled the gables, clawing for footing like lumberjacks riding great log rafts. And most of them lost to the rivers in the end. Sometimes men rode the drifts, hung to a house roof, unwilling to give their life's work up so easily to the rivers. They would stay with their house until it beached, and then they sat on the river muck trying to think of a way to work the house back upriver. There was even a breed of men who watched along the rivers ready to swim out and claim the lonely houses that fought the currents alone and abandoned by owners. They rode the houses to their end and salvaged what they could.

Bloated livestock bobbed along the surface of the rivers. More than once a horse's mane was mistaken for the hair of a human and people followed it along the bank, pulling at it with long poles, trying to lodge it in the tops of the willows that quivered and sang a weird song to the currents. And then, recognizing it as a horse, they would leave it to the river and the crows and buzzards who came and picked the hide and flesh from it. Often the bones lodged in the tops of the willows and when the rivers fell the sun bleached the bones until they were as white as a cloud.

Many people lost their lives to the rivers during flood. Some were found, others were not. Bodies were pulled to shore, tied to a willow and left there until identified. All were eventually given a Christian burial. Many times by strangers, and often the names of the dead who were buried were unknown. And for those that were never found, kin gathered along the rivers after the water had subsided, searching the brush, following the crows and buzzards, giving up in the end and throwing wreaths of flowers to the currents, hoping that the rivers would carry the flowers over the watery graves of their dead.

We huddled inside the river shack eating meagerly so that the small amount of food we had would last the flood. Often it didn't, and Pa paddled his joeboat to land and searched for food to bring back; and often he paddled into the currents and caught chickens, dressing them before he reached the house and little Arlie had a chance to make a pet of them. Arlie would not give a live chicken up; he would tack a name onto it at sight, and if in the end he lost the chicken, he refused to eat it.

At times when Pa caught more chickens than he thought we would need, he would paddle to other river shacks that still stood and divide them with the people there, always claiming that they were much less fortunate than we were.

When the water began to fall we followed the slow pace of the rivers, scraping and chipping at the muck left behind, stirring it into mud soup and pushing it into the rivers to be carried away by them, not us. For if we failed, the wind and sun would set the muck until it became as hard as concrete. While we fought the river muck we watched the long lines of mule-drawn wagons pass on their way back upriver loaded with plunder gathered farther downriver. Some of the plunder belonged to the drivers, some was salvage, and some had even belonged to us before the rivers claimed it. Sometimes little Arlie recognized our plunder and John and I would have to wrestle him to the ground to keep him from trying to pull it from a wagon.

Arlie was too young to know that such plunder was a gift of the rivers. A fair exchange enjoyed by river people, and especially by us. Often, we chucked plunder from our house that was worthless, or that Ma had grown tired of, in exchange for something that was better or, for Ma, just different. All kinds of things came floating past. Pa kept a long rope with a set of hooks on one end for just such a purpose. Pa had only to climb to the attic, open the hatch, stand on the roof, and throw the hooks into any object that floated by that he wanted. Pa could throw the hooks with the skill of a headsman on a paddle-wheel boat. And if the plunder was farther out than the rope could reach, he paddled his joeboat after it, often taking John and me with him and leaving little Arlie screaming at the window.

We often watched the rivers at night with a lantern. And sometimes Pa would set the hooks into a log and leave the rope out overnight. The log would create a drift and worthwhile things would catch in it. John would get mad and pout because Pa wouldn't allow him to dive into the river and swim to the drifts instead of taking the joeboat. John claimed he could swim like a muskrat and he wanted to show somebody, especially Pa. Little Arlie always enjoyed the argument, especially since John always lost. This was one of the few ways in his world he could get even with John for keeping him from doing the things he wanted to do and John was set by Ma to guard to see that he didn't. To little Arlie it was always John and never Ma.

The exchange system worked out very well over the entire course of the years. Some years were good, others bad, but in the end everything equalized. For Pa and Ma it was always household plunder, much of which Pa sold in his secondhand store. Mostly for John and me it was good lumber to build a better tree house where we could sleep sometimes during the warm summer nights listening to the winds quarrel among the willows and the wash of the waves from the paddle wheels.

When the rivers were back within their banks we went for long hikes along them, treasure-hunting for miles, searching drifts and the tops of willows. John always looked for the drifts caught in the forks of willows. And he scooted to the tops of the trees, often far above the drifts, Ma scolding as he blew in the wind like a squirrel, wanting, I think, more to show off than to search the drifts for treasure. Little Arlie walked until his legs gave out and then we took turns about carrying him on our backs; him kicking and screaming to get down, but unable to walk if he did.

Pa believed that we held an advantage living in the old river shack that stood near the mouth of the little river. He conceded that the Ohio was the mightier and held more plunder. But, being broader, the great Ohio was a slow riser and people living along it had more time to secure their plunder from the currents, or to move them to higher ground. The Sandy was more treacherous. Its many feeder streams could swell the smaller river out of its banks within hours, forcing people along it to move fast, often giving up their more valued items. And then there were those who were careless, those that had not learned to love the rivers and so could not judge them. This was especially so, Pa believed, among the wealthier folk that lived higher on the banks. They did not have reason to be as close to the rivers as the river people in the shacks along the shore. Pa believed you had to live with a river to know it. And Pa's knowledge often brought both fine plunder and dignity to the old house.

There was still another advantage the two-story river shack held that Pa seldom spoke about. We did not own our house. Few of the river people did. Not because the shacks themselves cost a good deal, but because the land they occupied was very valuable since the day would come when industry would move into the valley and build on the land along the rivers. Industry would need the land because it offered access to the rivers that would furnish transportation for them. The land was now owned by wealthy landowners who lived in the town and rented the river shacks for enough to pay the taxes on the land while they waited for industry more often for enough for their taxes and a profit besides. Pa's knowledge of the rivers paid off the day he rented the old river shack. He stood squinting at the crooked house and said to its owner, "I've never seen a house so crooked and still standing. I doubt it will stand another year against the rivers. A man ought to be afraid to live in a house like that. I don't think you could rent the house to anyone." And the landlord, sensing now not the loss of profit but of even tax money, shuffled his feet nervously. "I could let it go mighty cheap," he said. "Well," Pa said, "I could be a fool, but I might go as high as ten dollars a month." And the landlord hurried to accept the offer before Pa changed his mind. Pa grinned, knowing that the old shack with its poplar timber joist would hold out against the rivers for a number of years to come; long enough for John and me to grow big enough to help with the moving out, and for little Arlie to be born there. If he had tricked the landlord with his knowledge of the rivers, he felt that it was all evened up by the landlord's willingness to rent the house to him knowing that it could topple over with his family inside.

And still another advantage to the old house was the encounter of the two rivers created a backlash, building whirlpools so powerful in time of flood that they pulled plunder into them from far out in the stream, sucked them under, and released them in the slow-moving current that ringed the eyes of the whirlpools, close enough for Pa to set the hooks into them.

In 1937 a great flood came to the valley. And we spent our last year with the rivers and river shack. The first rise of the great flood was slow, and at first it looked like a bumper year for us. John and I sat at the table on the second story making our wishes for what we hoped the rivers would bring, just like we did every year. John wished for a joeboat of his own, and I wished for half interest in it and also a bigger bed since John was crowding me out of the one we were sleeping in almost every night now. And then little Arlie fooled us all. Maybe we had been too busy with ourselves to notice that he was growing up. He said, "I want the rivers to bring me a rocking horse. I can't bring the backs of the willows into the house with me and I like to ride."

In the days that followed Pa paced the floor restlessly, making many trips to the window, looking at the rivers and the sky. The rivers had risen and many of the townspeople had started moving to the hills. And then on the third day the rivers started receding and the people started moving back. But still Pa watched the rivers nervously. He was matching his great knowledge against them now. The rivers began another slow rise and then fell again. Pa shook his head. He said to Ma, "Choose what plunder you value that you think we can carry. I'll try to find us a house to rent along the foot of the hills while the people are moving back. It will be easier to find one now. I don't like the signs that I see and know. The hills have been heavy with snow over the winter; the earth is heavy with water yet to empty into the rivers. And the house won't beat the rivers this time."

Ma never questioned Pa. She began to bundle our plunder, showing face pains as she tried to decide what she could keep and what she must give to the rivers.

John and I helped, and while we worked tried to talk Ma into allowing us to keep what we knew in the end we couldn't. Little Arlie spent most of his time near the window, standing in a chair and looking out over the fast-rising rivers. And he kept asking Ma, "Won't the rivers give me my rocking horse before we go?" And Ma spoke to quiet him and keep him out of our way. "Just keep watching the rivers from the window, Arlie."

The current of the great Ohio had all stopped rising. The river heaved at the banks, like a huge, brown animal. And the water from the little river poured into it. Little Arlie stood at the window, leaving it only to

eat and sleep. He was the first one up now at daybreak, taking his place at the window, his mouth
puckered, rubbing his eyes from the glare of the muddy water. At nights he went to bed crying, afraid that
a rocking horse would pass during the night and he
would miss it.

Now the rivers began to crawl slowly toward the
town. Pa did not sleep. He lay across the bed with
only his shoes off, getting up frequently to stare at the
rivers. And then one night he walked to the window
and found Arlie asleep in the chair. Arlie had sneaked
out of bed that night and had tried to stay awake and
watch the rivers that were now high enough to touch
the house.

"Tell you what, Arlie," Pa said to him, "you get
your sleep and we'll just set us a fishing line outside
this window to catch that rocking horse if it comes
by."

And with Arlie making a promise that he would not
sneak to the window at night to watch the rivers, Pa
tied a hook on the end of a cord and dropped it out
the window into the muddy water of the rivers.

When morning came Arlie was the first one to reach
the window. He pulled at the cord, and tears welled in
his eyes when the empty hook caught on the sill of the
window. Pa threw the line out again. And he watched
the rain that was falling harder now. Evening came and
he said to Ma, "We'll move out at daylight and camp
along the foot of the hills until I find a house. We
can't stay here any longer." And Arlie ran to the window, doubled up his small fist and shouted, "I hate you
rivers I hate you rivers!"

That night I overheard Pa as he said to Ma: "I just can't leave having little Arlie hating the river like that. Thinking that the rivers have brought things to John and Simon and nothing to him."

"But the fishing line won't catch anything but drift," Ma said. "You know that."

"I know," Pa said.

"Where are you going?" Ma asked.

"Down to my workshop before the water is too deep there," Pa said.

I heard Pa working long into the night below us, sawing and hammering. Once I looked through the cracks in the floors and saw him there, water waist-high, beside his workbench, wood in his hands, taking shape now.

Just before daylight he came back upstairs. He was carrying a crude rocking horse in his arms. He walked to the window and set it there while he pulled in the fishing line. He tied the line around the rocking horse and lowered it out the window.

Arlie woke us all at daylight. He had his hands on the fishing line, his feet braced against the wall, pulling and hollering for all he was worth.

Pa hurried to the window. He said, "What you got there, Arlie? Here, let me help you." And Pa took the line, pulled it until the head of the rocking horse showed above the sill of the window. Seeing the horse's head, Arlie got so excited that he lost his hold on the cord and went sprawling into the center of the room. He got to his feet, screaming, and headed back to the window. He grabbed the horse around the neck and Pa pulled them both into the room. "I'll be doggone!"

Pa said. "Look what the rivers have brought to Arlie!"

The rivers were high on the sides of the old house now and we could feel a slow sway in the floor. We crawled from the window of the house into the joeboat and Pa paddled toward high ground. I quarreled along with John because the rocking horse that Arlie still held around the neck took up so much room in the boat. But little Arlie paid us no mind; he had Ma and Pa on his side and he knew it. He looked at his rocking horse and then at the rivers. "I love you rivers," he said. And then he looked toward the old river shack fighting for its life now against the swift currents. He said, "And I love you, too, old house."

The rivers claimed the old house that year just like Pa said they would; lifted it from its footing and carried it to its watery grave.

3.

The Naming of Mr. Creighton

LEIF Hager was the goshdangest man to get a nickname stuck on a fellow you ever saw. I mean the thing was, Leif never gave you the name himself; he'd set his sight on you and he had this knack of coming up with something that was sure to cause the other fellow to do it and leave Leif with the credit. Leanbird, Bushhog, Carbuckle, Cowhock—them's some first handles to have to carry to the grave with you. None of us liked them, but we couldn't shed them, and I guess he had just about got us all except Mr. Creighton. And, well, we figured Leif hadn't shied away from Mr. Creighton for twenty years for nothing. I mean Mr. Creighton just wasn't the sort of man who's easy to put a nickname on—deserving—but more than a match, even for Leif. I guess that's why it struck up such an interest around Sourwood the day Leif started paying Mr. Creighton a little more attention than usual. And when he took to watching his habits and whereabouts, things changed to being right down exciting—enough to wager a few bets on.

Mr. Creighton was a hard case. A little weasel-eyed man who wore glasses thick as a soup spoon, always walked around town wearing a suit and tie and carried a pearl-handled cane that he'd strop you with if you called him anything but Mr. Creighton. Demanded dignity and claimed respect was due him; and he got it because you knew he was the sort that would call the law on you if you as much as laid a hand on him; just uppity the worst you ever saw a man be.

Mr. Creighton claimed he had been something and then some back in the early nineteen-hundreds when they were bringing logs down the river and Sourwood was a boom town. And there wasn't anyone around to tear down his story since Ringtail Sawyer had died some years ago. The town dried up when the timber went and most of the timbermen had either left town or stayed on and died off. But Ringtail used to say that he didn't recollect Mr. Creighton being anything special when the logs were on the river; except a little more cautious than most men, being he was so little and ribbly; wore a suit and tie even back then, though, and Ringtail had heard he made his living by ciphering books. Mr. Creighton had even had his cane back then, Ringtail said, but he hadn't been so ready to strop a man with it as he was now, which figured out all right. I mean there were half men and half alligators walking the streets back then, rowdy and searching like buzzards for something to pick on.

Well, Mr. Creighton had been something. And he had made a little money and had known how to hang on to it. He lived with the fool notion that the logs would come again to Sourwood, and the town would boom. He still claimed he'd be in on the first log and make a sack of money. And it took nerve to believe that. Meanwhile he just went around stropping you with his cane if you didn't watch out, and being called Mr. Creighton.

Well, the man who took the blunt of the blows from Mr. Creighton was Beans Dawson. Beans had the only restaurant in Sourwood that run full time, and it was where Mr. Creighton ate, three meals a day.

Beans had mostly beans on his menu. In one form or another it was beans for breakfast, beans for dinner and beans for supper. I mean that's what you got if you made it through three meals a day. Aside from Mr. Creighton, Beans took what little trade he had from people passing through.

I guess being set in his ways was the worst fault Beans had. He had speculated by buying up a wagon-load of commodity beans when the government had passed them out to the people during the '30's, and had set his mind to getting his money back. It couldn't of been much money; not nearly as much as Beans claimed. I mean the people got the beans for nothing toward the end, twice as many as they needed since the government claimed it cost more to transport the beans out when it was over than it did to leave them in. And the people sold the beans to Beans for little or nothing.

Well, Beans done all he could as far as the beans were concerned. He had spent most of his time since the '30's trying to come up with different ways he could serve them. He boiled them, baked them, roasted them, fried them, and even had a fancy dish he called bean soufflé. I don't think it ever really amounted to much. I mean a bean ain't much to work with, especially a white one.

Having Mr. Creighton for a steady customer for so many years wasn't an easy life. Mr. Creighton ate like a canary bird, which didn't make much of a dent in the beans, and he was picky, demanding of respect, and slung insults at Beans ever-which-way over what he did eat. Mr. Creighton claimed that it was he who was mostly keeping Beans from having to close his doors, and that entitled him to more than he ever got. To say nothing of helping Beans get rid of a bad speculation he had made back in the '30's.

Catching Mr. Creighton's habits or whereabouts wasn't hard to do. He lived mostly alone in a big thirty-room building that stood over near the river and had been a hotel back when the logs were on the river. Finest this side of Louisville and Cincinnati, they said. He had a room on the top floor where he could look out over things and complain once in a while about the mission they opened up sometimes on the first floor where the saloon used to be, claiming the noise kept him awake nights.

He was up every morning at six, dressed in his suit and tie by six thirty and on his way to eat breakfast by six forty-five. It all put a considerable strain on Beans since he had always wanted to sleep late and didn't like frying beans that early in the morning. But

Mr. Creighton was a steady customer and had the money to pay and Beans *had made* the speculation.

The thing was, Beans couldn't set a plate out to Mr. Creighton like he would to an ordinary customer and ought to have had the right to do being he owned the restaurant and all. Each morning it was the same ritual: he had to stand beside Mr. Creighton's table like he was nothing but a common waiter instead of the owner of the place, waiting for Mr. Creighton to scan the menu, as if it had just been written up when it was the same menu he had been looking over the years. And none of this was at the counter where the singles and strangers who came in to eat sat; Mr. Creighton would have to dirty a table that Beans tried to keep clean in case families ever stopped, and he'd prop his feet on the rungs of the chair, which scared it considerably, stick out his little chest and say, "I think I'll have fried beans and coffee." And there'd go Beans' clean tablecloth.

Beans would take his order, and then he'd have to make a trip to the counter to get a newspaper that had come up from Cincinnati so long back that the pages had yellowed and hand it to Mr. Creighton to read while he sipped at his coffee and waited for the beans. Mr. Creighton squinted at the paper through the soup-thick glasses like the news was hot enough to burn.

When the beans were served he'd hand poor Beans the paper back and sling insults. "Why don't you get a newspaper that's got something in it? They don't know nothing about putting out a paper down there in

Cincinnati; they're even dumb enough to say that the logs are gone from the river for good. That's how much they know about it."

Well, like I said, Leif had at long last put his eye on Mr. Creighton, and the way it turned out he made his first move at Beans Dawson's. Leif lived outside of town on Paddlecreek, and one morning while he was coming to town with a bucket of berries to sell he stopped along the creek, spotted a coot bird swimming in the water, and blowed its head and right leg off with one shot. He polled it to the bank and looked it over. "Well, you look something like a duck," he apologized.

Then Leif set about to dress that bird up a little. He picked it clean as a creek gravel and brought it in to Beans Dawson's restaurant. "Yep," he says to Beans, "he's a fine-looking duck. Fresh and right out of my own stock."

"He's sorta small, ain't he?" Beans said.

"Small and tender as a bloodroot," Leif said. "A little bird like this would sure lay down the hackles of a rowdy customer."

I guess that part about laying down the hackles done it. Beans was all smiles. He had just the right customer in mind; yes sir, Mr. Creighton. He'd not only hang up the old man's cane, but he'd give the old man something that would stay with him for a while. He'd do this bird up right. Serve him under glass like he had heard the old man say they did in the swanky places in Cincinnati and Louisville. And sometimes as far north as Boston, Mr. Creighton had said.

It took Beans all morning to fix the bird. But he was ready and making a trotting noise across the boards of the counter with his fingers when Mr. Creighton walked in at noon, swinging his cane and looking around like he was searching for something to swing at.

Beans waited until Mr. Creighton was seated since you chanced a blow from the cane if you approached him for his order beforehand, and he handed him the menu—a menu that had the beans dropped to the bottom while taking up the center of the sheet was: ROAST DUCK—UNDER GLASS.

Well, I guess Beans was really expecting something from Mr. Creighton and all he got was a big letdown. I mean Mr. Creighton just demanded the morning paper and said, "Egod, Beans, I see my coming in here three times a day for the past twenty years has rubbed off some on you. I'll have that roast duck under glass and hope that my stomach can adjust to the change."

Beans brought the small bird out on a tray and under a large fishbowl beer mug, which was the best he could find. And then he walked back to the counter to figure up the bill. Now and then he glanced at Mr. Creighton, hoping to see some sort of appreciation on his face. And finally he saw Mr. Creighton looking deadpan straight ahead and waving him over to the table with his little bird-claw finger. Beans hurried over.

"Something wrong?" Beans asked.

"This here duck," Mr. Creighton said, pointing his

fork now at it. "Unless my eyesight fails me I see only one leg sticking up from this bird. You wouldn't be trying to pass a cripple off on me, would you?"

Beans looked at the one puny leg on the bird and scratched his head. He said:

"You ain't the only one that eats here. Some of my other customers like duck too."

Mr. Creighton said:

"You get this straight. When I order duck I ain't looking for scrappings. If you sold off part of this duck you should have let the neck go. Leg is choice. Don't you forget that I'm the best customer you got. I'll have my coffee warmed up."

Well, by 12:15 the bird was a skeleton out from under glass and no bigger than a man's fist. At 12:20 Mr. Creighton walked out of the restaurant right on time. And Leif was there, leaning up against the front of the building.

"Howdydo, Mr. Creighton," Leif said, with a respectful air, "and how are you feeling today?"

"Never better, thank you," Mr. Creighton said, twirling the cane with one hand and patting his stomach with the other. "Just the way a man should feel that's been eating beans for twenty years and then dines on duck under glass. And how are you feeling today?"

"Fitter than usual," Leif said. "I've sold off a bucket of berries and a coot bird already today, and the sun's still noon high."

"A coot bird!" Mr. Creighton said. "Who in the world would buy a coot bird?"

"Well," Leif said, "Mattie Toliver took the berries and Beans Dawson the coot bird."

"Beans Dawson the coot bird!" Mr. Creighton said.

"Promised it to him the other day," Leif said. "Beans says to me last Thursday, 'Leif, bring me in a good-sized bird corpse when you can. I got these big river rats coming up from the river again trying to gnaw into the room where I keep my beans stored. I'll soak the bird in pizen and get rid a few of 'em.' 'That ought to do it,' I says to Beans. Well, I brought the corpse in this morning. Caught me a good-sized coot swimming in the backwater over on Paddlecreek and blowed his head and right leg off with one shot. Long shot, too. Dressed out just like a little duck."

"Right leg off!" Mr. Creighton said, leaning against the building. "Are you sure about the right leg and the way he dressed out?"

"Well, yes," Leif said. "I remember particularly the fuss Beans made over the bird's having one leg gone. I couldn't see that it ought to make a difference but Beans said the rats were coming and plenty. And he wanted to do this job up right."

Mr. Creighton was trembling now, holding to the cane and building for support. He was as pale as a summer cloud.

"Why, Mr. Creighton," Leif said, "ain't you feeling well? You've turned awful white all of a sudden."

"Get me to the doctor, young man," Mr. Creighton said. "I've just been poisoned."

"Poisoned?" Leif said. "What makes you think that?"

"Don't argue with me at a time like this," Mr.
Creighton said, trying to raise the cane but dropping
it back down for support. "Beans Dawson has poisoned
me with a coot bird; passed it off as duck. Probably
had it all planned for years now. Not a respectable
bone in his body. Hurry! The doctor, quick!"

"But it could have been a duck," Leif said. "Course,
Beans has been acting funny here lately, but he surely wouldn't go to something like that."

"A duck with its right leg gone!" Mr. Creighton
said, trying to wobble off. "Why, it wasn't no bigger
than a mud hen."

"We better get started!" Leif said.

Well, the doctor in Sourwood meant one man:
Tom Dinkle. Butcher Dinkle, he was when his back
was turned or you wasn't needing him for ailments.
Doctor, lawyer, dentist, preached on the side: you
name it and Dinkle had the shingle to hang up. When
you went inside his office you met his wife sitting behind a desk and acting as his secretary. Her name
was Miss Rankins while he was on duty, which was
her maiden name, because Dinkle thought a secretary
ought to be some removed from the boss. It was more
businesslike and worked out better all around. And it
was the secretary's job to check out anyone that came
in the door; I mean what their business was: ailing,
legal matters, toothache, or a preacher to confide in.
It had to be this way. Dinkle claimed that people
had come to see him before he got his secretary and
took advantage of him. I mean they'd come in to see
a preacher when they really had ailments and some-

where during the confiding they'd try to worm out a cure for their ailments. And there was a heap of difference in the price. I mean he could set a fee on it for doctoring, but had to take an offering for the confiding. So the way it was now, Dinkle stayed off in a back room or went there when he saw someone coming, and his wife got the lowdown and took it to him.

Leif busted in the door and Miss Rankin stuck one leg out so he couldn't pass and said:

"Nature of your business?"

"Good Lord, lady," Mr. Creighton said, "Don't waste time, I've been poisoned!"

Miss Rankin jumped from her chair and hurried toward the little room in the back shouting, "Doctor, doctor, emergency!"

Dinkle stuck his head in the waiting room door and motioned Leif and Mr. Creighton back toward the other room. Mr. Creighton was wobbling something awful now, and Leif staggered with him, got him to the room and dropped him down in a chair. Dinkle, wearing a white jacket, looked down at him.

"What's bothering you, Mr. Creighton?" he asked.

"Poison!" Mr. Creighton said. "Beans Dawson has just poisoned me on a coot bird." Mr. Creighton managed to draw his mouth down. "Passed it off on me as a duck."

"Well," Dinkle said, "you don't look like a man what's been poisoned to me."

"How can you tell from up there?" Mr. Creighton asked.

"For one thing," Doc Dinkle said, "you ain't slobbering at the mouth." And it looked for a minute like Mr. Creighton might get a heap better. But I guess Doc Dinkle sensed it in time. He added, "Course, the lack of slobbering don't always mean the lack of poisoning. And a doctor has got to be sure. After all, that's what people come to see a doctor for. And pay for.

And with Mr. Creighton trying to break Dinkle's neck hold, Dinkle poured a half pint of caster oil down him. Mr. Creighton shook his head a few times like a chicken trying to knock something loose that's stuck to its bill. He finally caught his breath. He said:

"If I ain't poisoned, I'll take Beans Dawson to court. There is a law against trying to poison a man. Ain't there?" And he was looking at Doc Dinkle.

"Well, now," Doc Dinkle said, "that's a little out of my line of doctoring. I'd say you ought to check that out with a lawyer."

"Maybe I should," Mr. Creighton said.

And Dinkle had shed his coat, put on thick glasses, and pulled up a chair.

"Now, then," he said, "let's see what sorta case we got."

"Well, he passed the coot bird off on me as a duck; that's one thing," Mr. Creighton said.

Dinkle rubbed his chin and studied. Finally he said:

"Well, it ain't all that easy. You ain't given me much to handle your case with. I mean after all, you've ate up the only evidence we had. You've ate the better part of the bird, and if I know Dawson he's already souped the bones into nothing."

Mr. Creighton was shuffling his shoes on the floor now.

"Well, what can I do?" he asked, desperate.

"It appears to me you got some confiding to do," Dinkle said. "Might as well have a look at your teeth while you're in here, too. But the confiding is always personal with me, just as it ought to be." He looked at Leif. "Would you leave us a while?"

Leif went his way and finally Mr. Creighton left. Dinkle walked out to his secretary and said:

"Make a bill for doctoring service, legal fees, dental work, and put a dollar on the books and mark it up to confiding."

"Yes sir," Miss Rankin said. "And who will I charge the bills to?"

"Coot Creighton," Dinkle said. "Who else?"

And the name stuck. Same as the names had on the rest of us.

4.

The Tale of Scrapiron Jack

HIS name was Patches, and he had grown old on the river. His skin was wrinkled and parched, and his hair matched the bleached driftwood boards that framed the shack under the willows where he lived. Two years ago his hearing had gone bad, and he had learned to use his eyes to read the signs of the river and the sounds from human lips.

The river was his only friend, and he had been talking to it for many years, both in silence and often loud enough to be heard by passersby. But now with his loss of hearing he could not hear the many answers that the river used to give. And he missed the low sounds of the waves washing against clawed tree roots and high mudbanks; the slow ripple of the water as it washed over the sandbar down from his shack, a sandbar that he had once kept clear of brush and snags and other debris washed in by the river. He kept his joeboat tied to the one great willow that occupied the bar. His eyes, although crowfooted heavily, had remained keen and he used them almost entirely now to read the signs of the river. He got many answers. Whitecaps spoke of coming rain, and blue water of good catfishing.

Signs meant his living. The trench cut in the sand and mud by the tail of the river turtle; the track of the muskrat and mink; and the color of the willow branches, water-soaked and white and flexible now to bend into willow chairs to sell either in town or more likely to the people on the paddle-wheel excursion boats that plied the river in the summer.

It was May now and Patches sat on the bowed back of an old willow that he used for a chair in front of his shack and looked out over the river. The wind had brought a restlessness to the surface of the water and the old man knew that rain was not far away. A warm wind lifted the tops of the willows along the bank and he imagined he could hear the quarreling of the leaves and the calling of the rain crow swinging on a branch and singing of rain. But he knew that he would never hear the wind or the song of the rain crow again. Puffing his pipe he watched the river breathe upon the sand like a great eel, in and out.

"River," he said, "it will be only a day or so before the rains come. And with the rains will come old Scrapiron Jack. He'll flip his tail, glide out of that big Ohio, and then belong to you. And again this year I'm waiting for him. This could be my last chance to catch him; I'm an old man. And as close as me and you are I cannot become a part of you. You can wash away the banks and then build them back up; wash out willows and then give water so that more can grow in their place, but you can't take the grayness from my hair or the ache from this old body. You never change. But my change is forever and I'm dead once. But of the things you have been able to give to me, you have shared them all but one—Scrapiron Jack. And I always reckoned if I lived with you long enough you'd give me him, too. I've lived with you a long time, River. What do you say this year?"

Patches studied the river closer.

"Take your time, River," he said, through puffs of smoke. "Take your time."

His thoughts now were of the big catfish Scrapiron Jack. A great catfish. And once the mention of his name would have told you so anywhere along the river. The fish had been hooked by a lot of fishermen, but he had never been held. Many fishermen had left a hook in his mouth, cutting the nib from their trotline to save it and then looked on in disgust and sadness and admiration while the great fish swam away. The hooks had given the old fish his name—Scrapiron. Patches himself had hooked him twice. Just two times in all those years. The first time the great fish had broken his trotline. The second time Patches had gotten the fish as close as his joeboat and then the boat was capsized. He had swam to shore but had lost his entire trot and one of his two boat oars.

Patches looked toward the mouth of the river where it emptied into the big Ohio. The fish was out there, bound to be. And then the old man shook his head and looked toward the willows along the bank.

He knew that he should be thinking of ways to make a living instead of how to catch a fish too old and tough to eat or sell. But whenever summer came to the river, and the big fish began to stir, the fever of catching him always returned. Not for the money he might bring if he were cut up and sold for a younger fish; the old man did not like to even think of killing the great fish—just to catch him and then decide. He and the fish had grown old on the river together and the fish had always beaten him. And there was the envy that the fish was closer to the river than he. The fish was the native and Patches the intruder. And yet, at least for now, the old man must forget the catfish. He had made little money over the winter, and the summer before he had sold but one chair. Life had become harder since the small boy, Jobe, had drowned at the sandbar. Although it had been but two years ago, it seemed like a lifetime to the old man.

Patches thought of the river two years before. The boys used to come to the river then. And often they stopped to watch the old man weave his fishnets and minnow seines, make nibs for his trotline and weave the slender willow limbs together to form a chair. Or maybe they just came to hear about the catfish Scrapiron Jack. For most of the old rivermen that once spent their days along the river trying to catch the fish were gone and few people now except Patches and the boys believed the old fish was still in the river, or, for that matter, ever really existed. Patches believed because he had seen; boys believed because of their want. But it was the sandbar that the old man kept clean that brought the boys to this spot along the river. It made an excellent swimming hole and the joeboat tied there an excellent diving board and float.

And then the boy, Jobe, had drowned. Patches had swum after him until his arms cramped; dived until his breath would not hold; and in the end had had to leave the limp body of the boy to the river. A week later the river gave the boy up. His body was found snagged on a trotline miles downriver in the big Ohio.

The boy's father, Tom Kirby, had come to the river, pointed his finger at Patches and said, "You killed my boy."

The words had remained with the old man a long time. And even now as he thought of them, he shook his head in pain. Why was he to blame for the death of the boy? He had loved the boy. And he had taught the boy as he had most of the others to love the river, not fear it as many of the people of the town who did not know the river did. Even Tom Kirby. Jobe had swum too far from shore and just could not make it back.

But Tom Kirby had declared the old man a menace, and he had sworn out a warrant that had brought the old man to court. He had been freed, but as he walked back to the river and in the days that followed, he wondered what he had been freed for. Boys were taught to fear him, to stay away from the shack where he lived; and parents scared their children into minding by threatening to take them to the river and into the grasp of the old man to be hurled into the river. In the end some men from the town came and heaped brush, broken glass and debris along the sandbar and in the water to make sure a boy could never swim there again.

All of these thoughts whirled in Patches' head and he struck out at the river:

"I thought you were my friend!" he said, as he spat into the water. "You took the boy, not me. I wouldn't harm anyone. I'm just a lonely old man waiting to die. Answer me, River!"

And then the scowl on his face changed to an expression of nothingness.

"Maybe you got no answer," Patches said. "Maybe it is the same as it is with an old carp that has had his blood sucked away by the leeches until he's the color of death and then is brought to the surface and washed into the brush and picked to the bone by the crows."

Two years had been a long time ago and the old man had become very lonely on the river. He had sworn that there would never be anything between him and the river again. And there had been nothing until the boy came.

Patches turned his eyes toward the yellow path that crawled through the willows, ice plant and bugleweed like a snake. He thought of the small boy who had come down the path a short time ago. The boy had stopped in a clump of willow saplings and stared at the shack and the joeboat. Patches had attempted to scare the boy back up the bank. But the boy only twisted back and forth and smiled.

The next day the boy came again. And while

Patches paddled his joeboat along the shore to check his turtle lines, the boy followed him along the bank, watching. After that the boy came every day. At last he came to the boat and Patches did not try to frighten him. His name was Shim and his parents had moved into town only recently from over at Hazard. And in the boy's face the old man saw the loneliness of his last two years. Maybe, he thought, the town had forgotten, or maybe the boy's parents didn't know or didn't care. Lost in the boy's companionship, Patches reasoned no more. The boy came now to sit on the boat and his interest in the great catfish Scrapiron Jack pleased the old man. Patches laughed along the river as the boy's eyes widened when a turtle was taken from a hook or a bluecat from the trot. And in a very short time he grew to love the boy as he loved the river.

But a week had passed now and Shim had not been to the boat. The old man was left only with reasoning. Maybe the boy's parents had heard of him from some of the people of the town. Maybe the boy had been told to stay away and he would never be back. Patches did not like to think of being left alone on the river, even though he knew the boy should have never been —he had even taken an oath against his being. And yet, even if the boy was gone, Patches knew that he could not stop. Being old still was living. The year-leeches had not sucked all of his blood, yet.

And so he looked again toward the big Ohio. It was time now to think of catching Scrapiron Jack. Maybe even drag him through the streets of the town. Maybe this would show them that the fish was not just in the old man's mind.

Patches walked into the shack and came back out carrying a bucket of soft crawdads. There was much work to be done. He had waited until late in the day to bait his trotline fearing that the carp and gar might strip the hooks before darkness came. It had been better to give the carp and gar chicken guts and liver and doughballs to feed on during the day when they mostly traveled. Soft crawdads were hard to find along the edges of the river and a catfish traveled better at night and would seldom pass up a soft crawdad.

Patches walked to the boat, placed the can of bait inside, untied the joeboat, shoved it from bank and stepped in. He paddled slowly upriver, watching the ripples on the water and the trees along the bank. Both showed him signs of rain. He watched the clouds and the shadows of the willows disappear from the surface of the river. He would be racing the rain in baiting the trotline. He pulled the boat toward the bank and stopped at a large snag that stuck above the river a few feet from the bank. He leaned over the side of the boat, dipped his hand and arm into the water, gripped the trotline that was tied to the snag and held it to feel if anything was out on the line. He felt only the current. He lefted the line above water, pulled, and moved out into the river, baiting the hooks as he came to them. Reaching the end of the trotline he pulled up the rock sinker that anchored it to the bottom of the river and paddled upstream against the current to stretch the line before he dropped it. A drizzle of rain fell as he dropped the sinker. By the time he reached the sandbar below the shack the rain was coming down heavy, and he missed the noise the rain made hitting the river.

With the rain darkness came early. And he sat inside the shack thinking of the rain and the catfish. If the great catfish came into the river he would not be apt to pass up the crawdads. The trotline would hold him, but how would Patches get Scrapiron Jack to the boat? Always he thought of this, with every raise of the trotline. And he grinned with his thoughts of trying to pull the big fish into his small joeboat. Although he thought of many ways, the old man knew there was really only one. And that was to cut the trotline, tie it to the end of his joeboat and paddle downriver to the sandbar. Here he could wrap the trotline around the great sycamore and hope to wear the fish down.

The rain beat harder against the side of the shack. Patches was tired. And thinking of the sound of the rain against the boards of the shack, he fell asleep.

When he awoke it was still dark. The rain was harder. He took his lantern from the wall, lit it, walked to the door and looked out into the rain. He lit his pipe and searched for signs that the rain might abate.

He couldn't see any and he knew that the trotline would soon have to be raised, rain or no rain. For the early morning hour, that time when there is both a mixture of night and day, was an excellent time to take fish. He would have to be sure there was bait on the hooks.

Daylight began to break but the rain did not slacken. He stepped out of the cabin with his can of bait, walked toward the joeboat and saw the drops of rain sizzle on the globe of the lantern and burst into nothing. He bailed water out of the boat with a rusted tomato can, shoved off and paddled upriver.

At the snag he stopped to bail again and then touched the trotline and held. At first he felt the quiver of the line made by the current in the river. And then there was a light jerk that he judged to be about halfway out. A small fish. He lifted the line from the water and pulled out into the river. He stopped at the first hook to rebait. When he reached into his can for bait he felt a hard pull on the trotline. Not a jerk; just a pull that carried the slack in the trot downriver. The rain had brought a stronger current to the river and Patches imagined a water-soaked log snagged on the hooks and pulling the line along the bottom. He fastened the trotline to the back of the boat and tried to oar upriver to unsnag the line. But the pull was too hard and he continued to lose ground and drift downriver. The trotline was swinging in close to the bank and Patches knew that once the log was able to anchor the line against the snag, the line could well break. The only hope he had to save his line now was to cut it as close to the bank as he could, tie it to the end of the joeboat, paddle downriver and try to loose the line from the other side. Then he could tie the trotline off and reset in open daylight. He looked toward the clouds hoping they might open up and let some light through for him to see by. The rope for a new trotline cost money, not counting the great amount of work in remaking.

He reached into his pocket and pulled out his knife. But as he started to cut he felt a jerk on trotline and watched it slowly move upriver against the strong current. And knowing that a log could not pull against the current, he blinked rain from his eyes and felt the slow, steady pull. His heart beat faster and he breathed harder. He knew what was on the line. He held onto the trotline and tried to think. He had waited and thought a long time about this moment and he knew that his only chance was clear thinking. He could lose it all in seconds. Think, old man, he thought. You know you can't pull the great fish to the joeboat with or against the current. Most of the advantage belongs to the fish. But Patches did have a chance—a good one: the fish must be hooked good or he would have been off the hook by now; and he could have been hooked long, perhaps early in the night, and be worn down some.

Patches used what slack he could gather in the line to get closer to the bank. And then he cut and quickly tied the trotline to the end of the joeboat. He set his oars in the water, took advantage of the current to get downriver and used its power to keep close to shore. The rain fell and once he took the can and bailed water from the boat. Slowly he moved, leaving some slack in the line to avoid putting pressure on the great fish and tempting a fight. The pressure and the fight would come once the trotline was tied to the willow below the shack.

Through the rain he could see the shack and he dropped one oar and guided with the other. The boat slid in to the sandbar and the old man untied the line and stepped quickly on the bar. He wrapped the line around the willow, secured it, and sat down in the wet sand and lit his pipe. The job was yet to come but he smiled at the thought of having the catfish on the line. If he could get the fish to the edge of the bank he had a chance to take him.

But the fish was not caught yet. Knocking his pipe against his leg, Patches stood, gripped the line and pulled slowly at the slack. When the line was becoming tight, he pulled a rag from his pocket and wrapped one hand with it. Once the pressure was put on the fish, the fight would come. And the fish would be fighting for his life. He stopped to rest his arms and think. And the line spun through his hands. He felt the burn of the rope but held tight. And then the line was jerked from his hands. But the willow held. The line moved up and down the river. And there was little Patches could do but wait. Daylight came, but it was a misty light. The rain was now a drizzle.

When the trot finally loosened, the old man started again to pull in the slack. And this time he wound the slack around a broken root of the tree so that it could not be taken away again. He sat down in the water, braced his feet against the roots and began to pull. And then the line went slack. Patches knew that either the fish was loose or he was swimming toward the bar. There was nothing he could do but keep taking up the slack. The line stopped and grew taut. The old man breathed hard and tried to wipe his face on his wet shirt. The fish was still on the line. How long it would take to wear him down Patches did not know. Or maybe the fish could outlast him. They were both old for the river. Patches felt his tired muscles and his cramped legs. He wondered if the fish was tired, too. The fish would not give up; he couldn't. And Patches knew that he himself would die holding the trotline if he had to. He wished that he could relight his pipe. And he thought of all the long days on the river during which he had dreamed of this moment. But now that it was here he felt more sick and tired than happy. Maybe he would lose the fish as before and he would be left once again with only talk of it. He thought again of his pipe. And then he thought of Shim. If the boy were here, he could light his pipe for him. And perhaps even see the big catfish.

But he knew that he must not think of these things. He must keep his mind only on the fish. There was more light now and he could see a distance across the water. He quickly judged its swiftness and then the length of the trotline still belonging to the catfish. Scrapiron Jack was closer than he had figured. His muscles ached but he pulled at the line.

Finally there was a break in the surface of the water and close to the sandbar he saw the blue tail of the fish. He watched him turn in the water and saw the whiteness of his belly. And he could see that the great fish was wrapped up in line and held fast. With a slow movement of his tail he moved with the line toward land. A few feet from the sandbar he settled to the bottom and did not fight the line any more. Patches looked down at him.

"Scrapiron," he said, "I got you at last. What have you to say to that?" And he laughed and his voice echoed along the river. He danced in the sand and then watched the old fish slowly open and close his mouth.

"Could you be trying to talk?" Patches said. "Are you cussing me or asking me to let you go? You would be cussing me, would you, you old fool. You're too tough and too much a fish to beg."

Patches studied the old fish closely now. And he watched the small circles of blood come from the fish's mouth and spread like red paint on the surface.

"I mean you no hurt," Patches said. "But there ain't nothing I can do to ease it. If I let up, you'll take advantage. If loosen the hook from your mouth you'll zip out into the current and be gone forever maybe." Patches relit his pipe and blew the smoke into the air. "And you, River. We are close, ain't we? You could have given this fish to many men, but you gave him to me."

The long black whiskers on the sides of the fish's mouth waved with the current. And the blood still came from his mouth, and Patches did not like to see the blood. The eyes of the great catfish showed no pain. He was truly a great fish, his size telling of his many years with the river. It is only natural, Patches thought, for a fish to bleed when there's a hook in his mouth. The fish is old, but he's lucky there is blood left in him; that the leeches have allowed him to live so long.

"You know what I'm going to do with you?" Patches asked. "Well, I'm going up on the bank and cut me a willow fork, run it through your gills and pull you from the river. Then, I think I'll show you off to the people in town."

As Patches walked to the shack he saw a movement on the path that led toward town. He stopped, squinted his eyes and saw that it was Sheriff Blain. Patches threw up his hand and waved and when the sheriff was close enough he said:

"What brings you to the river, Sheriff?"

"I'm afraid I got a warrant for your arrest, Patches," the sheriff said. "You better come along. I'll explain on the way."

Patches looked at the sheriff as if he might have misread his lips. But the expression on the sheriff's face told him that he hadn't. Patches looked toward the sandbar and then at the rope tied to the willow.

"But I can't go right now, Sheriff," Patches said. "I got to—"

The sheriff did not let him finish. He said, "We better move now. Some of the men are beginning to gather in town and I don't like the looks on their faces."

He took Patches by the arm and turned up the bank.

Once Patches was inside the jail cell, the sheriff sat down to talk. The boy Shim was missing. Had been gone since early morning. His parents had gone looking for him and had been told that he had been seen going toward the river, where he had been forbidden to go a week ago when his parents had heard all the talk about Jobe Kirby. And, well, in the excitement the parents had sworn out a warrant. The sheriff had rather welcomed it. The old man was safer in jail until the boy was located.

There was one small window in the jail, and through it the old man could see the black clouds gathering anew in the sky. Rain was coming again. A hard storm. And he thought of the current that would come to the river and of the old fish tied near the sandbar. Now Patches was as helpless as the great fish.

Not only did the old man feel the loneliness of the cell, but he felt the freedom that had been taken from him. And it was not of his doing. He knew nothing of the boy. Of one thing he was certain: if the boy had came to the river it was not in the area of his shack. But he worried about the boy. He had visions of his limp body being carried by the current. And he felt sorry for the great fish that had not even known the respect of being pulled quickly from the river and a sudden death. He would die so slowly now.

The rain came and it was late in the day before the sheriff returned to his cell. He opened the door and grinned down at Patches.

"You're free to go, old man," he said. "They located the boy. Sneaked off and made his way over to Hazard. Stopped at a cousin's over there and they got word back to his pa. You can stay until after the rain if you like."

Patches walked from the cell and stepped out into the rain. He turned toward the river, and he did not stop until he was standing staring at the big catfish, opening its mouth and holding on for whatever was to come. The bleeding from its mouth had stopped and the old man was glad. He took his knife from his pocket and stepped into the water. He touched the catfish and it settled again along the bottom.

"I'm sorry, Scrapiron," he said. "You don't belong to me. The people in town don't deserve to see so great a fish. You belong to the river, like me."

And with his knife he cut the old fish loose. But the fish was exhausted. It did not move. Patches nudged it.

"Go on," he said, "before I change my mind."

The tail of the catfish brushed his leg, and it swam out of sight toward the center of the river. The old man lifted his hand and yelled into the rain:

"Maybe I'll be after you tomorrow."

But tomorrow would take care of itself. The old man was tired now, and he turned to the shack to find rest.

5.

Clinton Takes a Drink

WELL, it all happened a few years back. Back when they were rafting the big logs up at the head of the Big Sandy River and drifting them down to its mouth at Sourwood. It was the spring of the year and the river was swollen by rains and muddy. It was time for the log rafts to begin coming down the river, and you just couldn't find a dog around Sourwood, leastways off of a chain. Folks around Sourwood had learned to judge the coming of the rafts by the fact that the stray dogs that hung around town all disappeared and lots of others broke chain trying to get away from town. The dogs knew when the logs were coming and for good reason. Big Jim Larkin, rowdiest of the timbermen, would be poling the first raft. And riding the logs beside him, hunkered, growling, and restless to leap to the bank, was his big walleyed wildcat, Sickem.

So the dogs scattered like buckshot before Big Jim tied off his logs to the willows and came up the bank leading that wildcat with a log chain. You could hear that wildcat hissing, sounding like a cold wind from the mountains, and see its head twisting from side to side as it looked for dogs. That wildcat hated dogs and it just easy-like bided time knowing like always that it would eventually find one loose, especially when Big Jim unyoked it from the log chain which he always did after he had been in town a spell. It was a pitiful sight to see: that big wildcat astraddle a dog's back and riding him off into the mountains.

Big Jim always spent his time in Sourwood at the same place—Dave Maddox's Trading Post. Dave had everything for sale from mule shoes to hard cider, one having about as much kick to it as the other, the mule shoes and cider, that is. The Trading Post stood overlooking the river along with a dozen other time-and-river-worn buildings, but it was the Trading Post that Big Jim singled out. Big Jim passed off reasons why he liked the Trading Post, including among them the cider. But Dave had different views of it, foremost among them the fact that he had once beat Big Jim out of over a hundred dollars in a casino game.

Now Dave was a man who appreciated a customer and all the business he could get. But a man with a wildcat on a log chain was something else. I mean it was always the wildcat coming in one door and the customers going out the other. Big Jim would tie the wildcat to a hitching post that Dave had mounted in the store to hang wares on, order cider, drink, and then look off toward the hitching post and say:

"Sickem, Sickem."

And while Big Jim always claimed he only called out the wildcat's name to settle him some, Dave, figured the opposite—and with a point. I mean "sickem" generally meant to tear in, and with the mention of the name the big wildcat would rear to its hind legs and leap at everyone inside the Trading Post, that is, what few customers were left. He seemed to sense that freedom was just a few mugs of cider away. Wall them eyes back and scream goose pimples over you, leap and tear and wrestle the hitching post. Longest teeth I ever saw on just one wildcat.

Big Jim could hold more cider than any man I ever knew. His stomach was round like a nail keg and must have been lined with sand. And somewhere during the day he'd always ease off to a hickory-barked chair that Dave had up for sale and doze while the sun was high. The wildcat would squat and stand guard, hissing and showing his teeth to Dave, daring him to come close to show the chair off to a customer.

The timbermen, after they had sold their logs, had money to throw to the wind. But Dave wasn't getting much of it. Almost every businessman in town was doing standing-room business except for Dave. Poor Dave. Big Jim sleeping in a hickory-barked chair, that wildcat hissing and striking at everyone who walked in, and Dave marking down the prices of his merchandise.

Well, that spring when the river swelled and circled the willows Dave sent word that he wanted to see me. And being that Dave had helped out out more than once by allowing credit, especially when I was grubbing it, I hurried to the Trading Post. Dave was leaned over the bar where he sold the cider talking to Chet Potter. He was stretching out his big arms and working his fingers to point toward the river. You didn't have to take one look to know that Big Jim would soon be tying off his logs and coming up the bank to the Trading Post.

Dave sees me come in and he says:

"Am I glad to see you."

"What's up, Dave?" I asked.

Dave slid me a mug of cider and said:

"Chet is threatening to bring that big bulldog of his over to my place today when the logs come in." And Dave winked at me on the sly.

I glanced at Chet. He was a little ribbly fellow with a long-beaked nose, beady-eyed like a crow. And he had a habit of coming to Dave's, ordering cider and pretending that it was more than cider and that he was among the big boys. He'd drink a little cider and get independent like he had the drop of power on something, his upper lip down and getting bigger and looser with each swallow of cider. And that was the way he was now.

"Look at'm!" Dave said, watching Chet swell out his little chest. "See. He's got the drop on me. For some reason he wants to sic that big, powerful bulldog of his onto the puny little wildcat of Big Jim Larkin's. And Big Jim the best customer I got!" Dave winked again on the sly and poured me another mug of cider.

Chet squinted his eyes, shoved his chest out until

you could see the print of his ribs through his shirt, and said:

"No use trying to sweet-talk me, Dave. Puny or not, it all makes no difference now. When it comes to my bulldog, Clinton, sympathy is out of the picture."

"That Clinton is sure enough some bulldog," I says, setting in to pay for the favors Dave had done me. "I'd hate to have that bulldog turned loose on me!"

"Me, too," Dave said. "I'll take that wildcat in my place any day over old Clinton, especially if that bulldog was feeling ornery."

Chet looked at me, swayed, burped and winked at the same time which was to say he figured he had Dave down for the count. He said:

"He's a dog all right. High-tempered, mean, and mite near like a son to me. I mean there ain't no secrets betwixt me and Clinton. We stand together. I tell him and he tells me."

"But you wouldn't have to tell him, Chet," Dave said. "I mean maybe not this one time—as a personal favor. Think of our friendship."

Chet rears back like he is going for an alligator, pops himself in the chest with his beesting fist, and says:

"And maybe have him find out one day from a total stranger! Nope. That dog is as sensitive as the skin on a shedding crawdad. Why, he understands most things like a human. I couldn't hold something this big back on him. Just don't push me, Dave."

Dave looks at me. "Threatening me with Clinton again," he said. And then he looks at Chet. "Now you ain't really meaning to bring that big Clinton over here to the Trading Post today and let him loose on that puny wildcat, are you, Chet?"

"Give me another cider," Chet says, "and give Rankin one, too."

"Anything you say, Chet," Dave said, pretending to be overobliging.

"Of course," Chet says, "I could change my mind." He wiped his mouth with his sleeve. He looks at me and then grins at Dave like a pumpkin what's cut out for Halloween. "I'm beginning to love everybody."

Dave flinches and sets out to backtrack.

"I appreciate that, Chet," he says. "I was hoping you wouldn't let all them low-down things that was said about old Clinton bother you. What of it if it was the worst sort of things I ever heard said about just one dog. I shouldn't of mentioned it at all. But calling old Clinton a *coward* just stuck in my craw. Doing something like that is just about as low-down as a man can get. And then, too, it was the way the fellows puckered their mouths and laughed when they said it."

Chet, hunkered down now, pops his head out like a turtle.

"Maybe I better hear it all just one more time," he said.

"It's the same as before," Dave said. "Some of the logging men stopped in this morning ahead of the rafts. Wanted to pick up a few provisions and asked me if I knew a man in Sourwood that owned a big ugly bulldog that went by the name of Clinton. I knew right off the bulldog belonged to you, and it sorta made

me feel proud thinking the fame of that dog had traveled so far upriver. I said yes. Then tell him, they said
to either get him out of town or start whittling a board
to stretch his hide on. Big Jim Larkin said that his
wildcat got a glimpse of that bulldog last year on his
trip downriver, and he ain't been the same since.
Pined away the winter and is acting up something awful now. That bulldog ought to have made himself
scarce last year. For it it's one thing old Sickem can't
stand it's an independent dog, especially a bulldog.
Says to tell the owner of that dog that if the mutt's too
dumb to get out of town, the least he can do is clean
him up a little so the wildcat won't dirty his teeth when
he slips the hide from his back. Old Sickem likes 'em
clean. And . . . now let's see what else they said . . ."
And Dave scratches his head like he is trying to call
back.

But Chet had heard enough. He shuffled his feet a
little and eyed the river.

He said, "I've been pushed to the brink, Dave." And
then he mellowed like a newborn babe. Tears came to
his eyes. "The abuse old Clinton has took at the hands
of Big Jim Larkin! Push no more, Dave!"

"Now, Chet," Dave says. "Who would believe that
that puny wildcat could shuck the hide from Clinton
like he was no more than a ear of corn? And who
would believe that you'd be afraid to bring Clinton out
during logging time? I mean just because he's always
tied up at home this time of year don't mean a thing.
He's a valuable dog. I wouldn't want to take a chance
on losing a dog like that myself."

"Them's all fighting words!" Chet said. "Fightinest words I ever heard!"

"Don't do it, Chet," Dave says. "If Clinton fights that wildcat, it's got to be at my place. Mainly because this is where the wildcat will be. Always is. I been watching you sizing up the Trading Post. Looking at the smooth floors and probably thinking how old Clinton wouldn't be apt to get paw-splintered here. And how you could ease the merchandise back and make room for a fight. Called a coward or not, don't do it, Chet. That ain't a bad little wildcat. Rowly sometimes, but it is an attraction of sorts and brings in a customer now and then."

"It's Clinton first!" Chet says, waving his pipe-stemmed arms into the air. "Keep my cider, Rankin, while I go for the bulldog!"

Chet heads out the door and Dave turns to me.

"Hurry, Rankin," Dave says. "Get to all the places in town and spread the word there's going to be one whopper of a fight at the Trading Post soon as Big Jim gets here. I've already took care of Big Jim. Sent word upriver this morning about all the things Chet said about that wildcat. Big Jim ought to be as mad as a wet rooster and raring to go by the time he gets here, which oughtn't to be more than an hour from now. I've got to get around to marking up the prices of my wares a little to compensate for furnishing the fighting pit and all. Ought to make a little profit."

"But what about that poor bulldog?" I asked. "That wildcat is sure to skin him out."

"Damn the bulldog!" Dave says. "I'm as tired of

hearing Chet brag about that bulldog as I am of having the wildcat here. Comes in here every day and buys a little cider, pushes out that biddy chest and it's Clinton this and Clinton that. Puckers his mouth and you and me both know they ain't enough strength in cider to put the wobbles to a tadpole. 'Don't push me Dave!' Why, they ain't a shove to the little runt. I'm tired of Chet's bragging ways and pretty near busted by the wildcat, depending on big business from the loggers each year which I ain't getting. Egod, I'll get something out of it this time. I'm tired of listening and close to bankrupt. But this time either the wildcat or bulldog will go."

Well, I passed the word the best and as far as I could, and I never saw so many people crowded in one store. Dave was working among them like a weasel, showing them the price of this and the price of that, selling an ax here and a piece of calico cloth there— and all of the stuff at a marked-up price. And he had an extra man selling outside to the people gathered on the sidewalk who didn't have room to get in.

Things were all set. Dave had moved some sort of wire contraption that looked like a cage into the center of the store, and he was all smiles. And sitting over in the corner on top of a keg of salt was Chet, a mug of cider in one hand and a chain that held old Clinton in the other. His hair was sticking straight up, and he had a wild look in his eye.

Then someone busted through the door and yells out that Big Jim is coming up the riverbank leading old Sickem. And then Big Jim comes busting through

the door. The wildcat winded the bulldog right off, and he leaped the length of the log chain in his direction, something fierce. Old Clinton lets out a mournful yell and leaps the opposite way. But Chet holds tights and checks him and then grins at the crowd, sitting there flat of his rump like a bullfrog and acting like Clinton is anxious to go the other way—toward the wildcat.

Dave gets Chet and Big Jim together, and they talk. And then Dave steps back and tells what they said. They have decided, Dave says, that the fight ought to be fought in rounds. It'll allow time for the sale of cider and merchandise which ain't no more than fair being that Dave is furnishing the place and all. Besides, fighting in rounds will allow everyone to see at least one of them. And Big Jim adds that since his feelings has been hurt, he favors rounds because it means that the bulldog will get a better whipping; and Chet thinks more time will bring about a better skinning of the wildcat since Clinton is somewhat out of practice.

After everyone had his cider and some little item or so from the store, Chet and Big Jim put the bulldog and wildcat in the cage and a yell went up. The fight was on. Or should have been. But, once loose from the log chain, the big wildcat took one leap to the side of the cage, bounded off like a coiled spring, and landed astraddle the bulldog's back. Clinton takes around the cage like he's standing on hot cinders, trying to shake Sickem, which he can't. He flops on the floor, rolls, and takes off running again. The wildcat is held solid.

Chet takes a good look, lowers his head, and Big Jim buys a piece of merchandise from Dave.

Well, if old Clinton wasn't a fighter he sure was gifted with wind. He carried that wildcat around and around the cage through six rounds, and the wildcat wouldn't even get off at the bell which was a brass spittoon that Dave later sold. They couldn't pry him loose, which didn't please Dave since he lost some sales. But they finally got old Clinton stopped running and he stood wheezing like a steamboat whistle, then flopped over on his side and stayed there. Chet was all sad and blurry-eyed. He walks up to Dave and says, "Give me a big mug of cider, the best you got." Dave pulls out a jug covered with river dust and spider webs. And I figure that Chet plans to drink it all, pretend a passout and miss the burial. But he don't. He made his way back to the cage and looked down at old Clinton, on his side now with the wildcat hooked to his back like he had been sewed on. Chet bent down, grabbed Clinton by the head, and poured every last drop of that cider down the bulldog's throat. Then Chet raised his head and said in a pitiful voice, "Water is the strongest he's ever been used to. Maybe cider will ease the pain and suffering."

But then old Clinton had jumped to his feet and as sure as a tadpole will make a bullfrog his eyes made a complete turn in his head. What little tail he had was standing straight as a poplar sapling. He sorta hunched his back and when he straightened up he threw the wildcat against the side of the cage. The wildcat hissed and tried to remount, but he couldn't do it. Clinton

just staggered into him, took old Sickem in his teeth
by the nape of the neck and flopped over with him.
Chet let out an Indian whoop and bought a horse collar which he didn't need since he didn't own a horse.

There was no use trying to get Sickem loose. Nothing worked. He was stuck in the bulldog's jaws like
bark to a tree. Big Jim dropped his head and sold off
the piece of merchandise he had bought from Dave,
at half price.

Finally the wildcat quit breathing. At least as far as
we could all tell. But Clinton still held tight. Just
closed his eyes and held on. After a long while Chet
and Big Jim got together and tried to figure out a way
to break the bulldog's hold. The wildcat was through,
but Big Jim wanted to take what was left of him
back upriver. But when dark came they wer estil studying, and Dave had put most of his merchandise on sale.
Chet said he figured the cider had done something or
other to the bulldog, and he'd probably let go when it
wore off. But they sat out the night, and Dave offered
a closeout sale.

Clinton opened his eyes at daybreak, but still he
held his hold. Chet took to pleading and begging the
bulldog, but the dog just walled his eyes at him and
whimpered. And then he started moaning and groan-
ing the likes you never heard. The crowd had dwin-
dled down to Chet, Big Jim, Dave and me. Big Jim
was humped up over the back of a chair eyeing the
cage, Chet and Dave were blinking their eyes from
lack of sleep, and I was swearing off being a part of
anything like it again. And over us all fell the mourn-

ful howls of that bulldog, slipping out from his closed jaws.

"Well," I finally said, "it's awful listening to that dog. Aint't there some way we can ease him some?"

And then Chet lifts up the spider-webbed jug of cider again and bends over the cage. That did it! I mean the bulldog came to the top of the wire for it, the wildcat dangling from his jaws like a wet rag. Since the bulldog still wouldn't let go of the wildcat, Chet pulls the dog's jowls open a little and lets the cider trickle in. The big eyes of the bulldog made another complete turn in their sockets, got caught wopsided, and then his lights went out. He flopped to his side as contented as a summer calf and let go of the wildcat. Big Jim grabbed the cat while he seen the chance, and he hurried out the door and over the riverbank.

Well, don't you know that bulldog took to cider like a water dog to water. I mean he was on it. Poor Chet. He tried to keep that dog in cider but nearly went busted after six months. And when he refused to buy, that bulldog got to coming to Dave's and pestering him and his customers. Just squatted there in the floor and let out mournful howls that put the shivers to you. As big a pest as Dave ever had. And then Clinton took a turn for the worse. When his begging for cider played out he took to nabbing customers by the britches and holding on until you poured cider down him.

One day Dave says to me:

"Rankin, I'm going to have to take action on that cider-drinking bulldog!"

"How do you mean?" I asked.

"Well," Dave said, "if I can't wean him, I'm going to have to maul the hide off him."

"Don't do it, Dave," I said. "That bulldog made you a wad of money once."

"He's got it all back and then some," Dave said. "I mean he's bankrupting me. Besides, what should it matter to you?"

"Well," I says, "in a way I feel to blame. I didn't get him the first drink of cider, but I got him the second. I mean when his moans got intolerable that morning I asked Chet to do something. And it was then that Chet come up with the idea to pour the second drink down him. That dog might have got over the first drink, but he learned if he held on he'd get a second. I've had a hand in bringing that bulldog to ruination."

So I put up a little fund for that dog then and there to pay for his drinks. And I kept it up until Chet got back on his feet and bought an apple orchard outside of Sourwood and the big bulldog took to spending his time watching the apples ripen.

6.

The Heart of a Woodsman

CALEB stood on the porch of the cabin where he lived and stretched his arms over his head as far as he could reach. He took a deep breath of the fresh, frosted air that crept down the side of the hill beside the cabin. He watched the wind tremble the limbs of the naked sugar maple in the yard, and then sing through the limbs of the trees farther up the hollow behind the cabin. The air was fresh and carried with it a scent of the pine that speckled the hills, and it brought new life to him.

Letting his arms fall to his side, he looked up the steep ridge. He set his eyes on the tall black oaks on top of the ridge stretching toward the clouds that hovered low, heavy now with snow. Below the oaks, lower on the slope, stood a grove of black walnut, and from this grove trailed a winding path of red clay, dodging blackberry bushes, weaving between scrub oak that still held dried leaves out to rattle in the wind, until it ended at the edge of the yard less than ten feet from where he stood.

Time had passed swiftly, he thought, since he had traveled up the path to the black walnut grove to gather the nuts. The first frost had come bringing ripeness to the walnuts that had been shaken from the trees by the wind and scattered over the ground. Caleb had gathered the walnuts into a heap and had trampled away the hulls that hid the thick brown shells from sight. And then pouring the hulled walnuts into a burlap sack, he had carried them down the side of the mountain to the cabin and spread them out on boards, keeping the nuts off the ground so that the wind could circulate underneath and dry away the stain as well as the dampness that now gathered in the winter winds. Dampness, he well knew, could seep inside the thick shell and spoil the rich hernel inside.

The frost had come late to the valley this year. And Caleb had watched for it, as restless as the wind. While he watched he dreamed of the three things he wanted most in the world. First, there was the metal sewing hoop for his mother to replace the worn and warped willow one she now used. This would come as a Christmas present. Next, and for himself, was the hunter's knife that lay inside the glass case at Tom Taylor's general store at the mouth of the hollow. And then there were the steel traps that hung from the nail on the wall in the store. Both the traps and the knife, he knew, were the marks of a woodsman. And this was his greatest dream of all: one day he would become the greatest woodsman in the whole valley. He would become even greater than his father . . . that is, greater than his father had once been.

Caleb thought again of the frost. There had been one advantage in its coming late. So near to Christmas the walnuts had brought a better price. The rich kernels would add a delicious flavor to Christmas candy.

And yet the money the walnuts had brought would not be nearly enough. It would be only enough to buy the sewing hoop with a small amount left over. The traps and the knife were still unearned, and there was little time left, especially for the traps. If he earned traps by Christmas Day, he would be late starting his trapline, for a good trapper here in the valley usually made his first set in early November. But the frost had been late, he told himself. The weather had been warm. Even if he could have started earlier, the pelts of the muskrats would have been blue and unprime. There was a chance now, so late in the year, that the hides would be red and prime. This he had been told once by his father at a time that now seemed so long ago, when he had been so small that he rode on his father's back over the deep holes in the creek on his father's trapline.

On a recent visit to the store he had stopped at a small grove of wild cherry that grew so close to the creek he could stand under the trees and hear the hum of the water, and he had examined the inner bark of the trees. The wild cherry bark here in the mountains sold for herbs and brought a fair price. But the bark was to strip from the tree, and in the winter bark did not sell for as much as it did when spring came and the sap was up in the tree. He had stripped a piece of the bark, chewed out the cherry flavor and stared toward the creek. The creek was as clear now as the winds of winter; as clear as the glass case at the store that enclosed the knife. As he stared at the creek, he imagined again he could see the knife. To begin with it had been shipped all the way up the broad Ohio River from Louisville. The handle was of hand-woven leather and had been hand-polished until it was soft as the bark of the summer sumac. The long blade was of the finest steel, blue as the blossom of the morning glory that climbed the stalks of autumn corn to peer at the sun. Tom Taylor had allowed him to hold the knife, and he had held it as gently as he would have held a bird's egg that had fallen from the nest. And holding it he had dreamed that he was the greatest woodsman in the whole valley. When spring came again to the mountains and the berries came to the wild ginseng, it would be so easy to slip the knife into the fertile loam and shove out the ginseng root to sell as herb. Last spring he had used a pointed stick. He thought too of skinning the bark from the sassafras root to use for making tea.

Then his mind had drifted from the knife, and he had thought of the traps that hung from the nail. They were not new traps, for they had known a few seasons. Perhaps they had belonged once to a great woodsman. The traps had been boiled in the bark of either oak or walnut, taking away the shiny color of the steel and the metal scent that might well scare away a mink who was much more cautious than a muskrat.

Thinking of the traps had sent a chill over his body; a chill that he reckoned came to the heart of all woodsmen. He thought of the muskrats that lived in the small creek and of their secrets he had learned when he had traveled the line with his father. They tunneled an entrance in the mudbanks under the surface of the water and hollowed out a hole higher in the bank where the water could not reach. Once the hole was dug they carried leaves of corn and grass into the hole for the nest for their young. Many times on his trips to the store he had spotted muskrat trails. And he had learned that the muskrat was careless and left his signs for a naked eye to see. Even if the muskrat chose to travel the water instead of the bank, his long, flat tail dragged the bottom of the stream and left a path to his home.

He thought of the times when he had been smaller and had sat in front of the grate fire back at the cabin and listened to his father's tales of the trapline. It had been then, Caleb thought, that he had become determined he would one day become a great trapper. Then he had been too young. Now he had grown until he was big enough to have his own line. But during this period of growing something had gone wrong. His father had stopped talking of the trapline, and then one day had pulled in his traps. And one night, shortly afterward, Caleb had overheard his father telling his mother that his trapping days were over. The traps had disappeared, and his father had spoken a strange word to him: conservation. Once his father had stood in the yard and making a sweep of his hand across

the mountainside he told Caleb that he hoped one day
his few acres might become a preserve. This would be
land on which all animals could live without being
hunted or trapped, at least until they had a chance to
become plentiful again. This, he said, was the meaning of the word conservation.

At least it was part of the meaning.

To Caleb his father had once been the greatest man
in the whole valley, the greatest of all trappers and
woodsmen. And then the word conservation had come
along. After that there had been nothing in Caleb's
mind but confusion. And then one day he remembered
the words that he had once heard from the lips of an
old hunter. The old hunter had owned the best coon-
hound in the valley and together he and the hound
had caught more coon than Caleb could count. But
one night the old dog had quit the trail and refused to
run. The old hunter had hissed him on the best he
could, but for the old hound the trail had ended. He
had quit.

"Lost his heart," the old hunter said, hanging his
head. "A hunting dog same as a hunting man is only
as good as his heart. Somewhere along the trail the
old hound has lost his. Now he's useless as far as the
woods are concerned."

Tears came to Caleb's eyes, and he was ashamed
of his father. But he bit his lips and became more determined than ever to become a great woodsman. Perhaps one day he would take up the trail where his
father had quit and he would travel it until it ended.
He would not stop. To him there was no meaning in

conservation. There was no meaning to anything that took away trapping and hunting. He did not have time to even think about the word. In his pocket were two dollars he had earned from the walnuts. One of the dollars had to go for the sewing hoop. The other dollar would not buy the knife, and it would make a mighty short trapline. His only chance was to buy the traps first and use the pelts to pay for the knife. He could do without the knife until spring . . . if only it wasn't sold before then.

Once he had thought of asking his father for money to buy the knife. But at the time his father had been preparing for a trip that would take him far up the Big Sandy River to cut timber, a trip from which he would not return until Christmas Day. Caleb knew that what money his father had would be needed to buy provisions to last him and his mother the winter through. He had walked a short piece down the path with his father.

"While I'm gone, Caleb," his father said, "you'll be the man at the cabin." He stopped to stare through the willow grove. "My being gone so far and so long and so often hasn't given us a great deal of time to talk, especially of my feeling for conservation. Perhaps I've only confused you and what I have to say now will also have little meaning. And maybe I know that whatever I say and no matter how many times I say it, it might still have little meaning. A woodsman must see with his own eyes to really believe. But while I'm gone I'd like for you to think about our talks. Perhaps you can think of them and compare all I've said to the field of corn we plant each year in the land along the creek below the cabin."

His father pointed toward the strip of land, although it could not be seen from where he stood. "Years ago, before you were born, your grandpa cleared that strip of land and planted it with a small sack of seed corn he had carried with him over the mountains from Virginia. At the end of the path he planted a small strip to use for seed, just like we do now. The next year he planted corn in the strip again, and the year after that and for many years to follow. And then one year the corn became thin. The stalks were no taller than you. It was called bumblebee corn because it was so short a bee was said to be able to reach the tassel without leaving the ground.

"Well, it took your grandpa a long time to figure out the trouble. But what he discovered and did make it possible for us to raise corn there today. He had worn the land thin, taking from it year after year, never adding or letting it rest to become fertile. And so one fall he gathered his seed corn into a sack and the next year he did not plant. He protected the ground from weeds and let it build back up. While he waited the winters were long and hard without corn. It was hard not to plant, especially since your grandpa was a farmer and loved the land. And he was an old man. In fact, he did not live to turn the land again. But the year after he left the valley I turned the strip and placed his small sack of seed in the furrows. And the corn grew so tall that you would have thought it would poke through the clouds where he could see it." The

wind became harder in the trees. "Think of the animals as you would think of the bumblebee corn.
They've been worn thin. It wouldn't be easy to allow
them to build, especially for a man who is anxious to
become a woodsman. But because your grandpa did
without in the last years, I had corn. And perhaps one
day when I leave the valley you won't have to learn
what the animals looked like from the pages of a
book."

Caleb stretched again and took another breath of
air. He glanced quickly down the path that led out of
the hollow. The wind was an evening wind and judging from the position of the sun above the ridge he
would have to hurry to make it to the store and back
before darkness came to the valley. He started quickly
down the path to stare once again at the knife and
traps and perhaps try to bargain with Tom Taylor.

Brushing aside the low-hanging limbs of the trees
along the path, he did not stop until he reached the
cherry grove. While he caught his breath he tore loose
a strip of the bark and began to chew out the wild
cherry flavor. And then he heard something splash in
the creek below him. Cocking his ear, he held his
breath and stopped chewing. He heard the patter of
feet on the dried leaves that the willows had spread
along the creek. Then it stopped. The world around
him became quiet.

Slowly he turned his head and looked in the direction from which the sound had come. Close to the edge
of the creek he saw the trunk of a large tree that had
been torn from its roots by lightning a few winters

ago. The tree lay silent, half of it across the creek and the other half on the bank. The swift current of the creek had torn away the bark as far up as it could reach, but where the tree rested on the bank mountain moss had sprouted along the trunk. The moss still held much of its greenness, making it look almost out of place in the brown world around it.

Caleb heard the noise again, coming from close to the log. Getting on his knees he crawled closer. And then he stopped. His eyes grew wide and he held his breath.

He watched the brown muskrat stick his nose into the air, look quickly along the bank and then edge closer to the log. Caleb looked at the long, flat tail, then at the body of brown fur and the long gray whiskers on the tip of the nose. It was enough, he knew, to satisfy any trapper, the biggest muskrat he had ever seen. And Caleb was so close he could see the whiskers blow in the wind that circled the log. His size told that he was an old rat, and his being on the creek said that he was also a smart one. He had not been caught.

The old muskrat reached his paw into the leaves under the log and pulled up a small crabapple, its brown skin wrinkled by the winter. He held the apple toward his mouth with his paws but just as he was ready to take a bite the apple rolled off and fell to the ground. The muskrat quickly scooped it up. And the apple fell again. The old muskrat twitched his whiskers as if he were mad and scooped the apple up again. But again it rolled away and Caleb heard it

thud in the dry leaves. A grin came to his face and
for a minute he thought he would have to laugh at the
old muskrat who could not hold the apple. He squinted his eyes and looked closer. And then the smile left
his face. And he knew now why the apple had rolled
to the ground so many times.

Caleb looked at the long claws on the right paw of
the muskrat. And then he looked at the left. Here there
was no paw, only a stub. There was only one thing
that might have taken the paw off the old muskrat:
the steel jaw of a trap. According to the tales he remembered from his father, this was not an uncommon
thing among trappers, especially bad trappers. A trap's
steel jaws could break the bone in a muskrat's leg and
with only the hide left he could twist away and gain
his freedom. A frown came to Caleb's face, and he
felt sorry for the old muskrat. He stared at the stub
paw again, determined to see it with the eyes of a
trapper. What did a trapper care whether a muskrat
had one paw or two? The paw was not left on the
hide anyway. But as Caleb stared at the paw he imagined the trapper who had once caught the old muskrat traveling to his set on a frosted morning and finding the paw in his trap. For a minute he felt angry at
this trapper. He could have been more careful, as
Caleb's father had once been. He could have made
the set where the water was deep and the weight of the
trap would have drowned the muskrat and he would
not have been left to travel the creek with one front
paw.

Caleb shook these thoughts from his mind and tried

again to view the muskrat through the eyes of a trapper. But somehow there was a difference. He had never
seen a living muskrat that had lost his paw. He had
never before seen an old muskrat struggle with a frost-
bitten crab apple that would probably pucker his
mouth even if he did have two paws to hold it with.
Maybe, Caleb thought, with only one paw the crab
apple had been all the old rat could find. And then
for some reason as he stared at the stub Caleb thought
of the bumblebee corn that had once sprouted in the
strip of land below the cabin. He imagined the stub of
the muskrat to be like the corn, short and useless. And
yet he knew that the muskrat's paw was much more
useless than the short corn. All the waiting in the world
would not bring the paw back to the muskrat.

Suddenly the old muskrat stuck his nose into the
air and turned toward Caleb. Caleb tried to edge closer
to the ground, but he slipped and fell against the dried
leaves. The old muskrat turned quickly and hobbled
toward the creek. There was a splash and Caleb
watched the ripples wash against the mudbank until
the surface was quiet and smooth. Then Caleb looked
over his shoulder at the sun and hurried on down the
path to the store.

"Back again, Caleb," Tom Taylor said, a smile on
his face, as Caleb walked into the store and stopped
in front of the case that held the knife.

Caleb squinted his eyes at the small, heavyset man
behind the counter. Tom Taylor had told him the price
of the knife before. But often Caleb had watched his
father bargain with Tom Taylor, asking him the price

of something again and again. Many times the last price had been less than the first. And if he was old enough to have his own trapline, Caleb thought, he was old enough to bargain too.

"How . . . how much did you say the knife was worth?" Caleb said.

Tom Taylor reared back and laughed.

"As much like your pa as two peas in a pod," he chuckled. "I see I got to watch or be skinned alive. Did I say . . . three dollars?"

A smile came to Caleb's face. The day before the price had been four dollars.

"I'm sorry, Caleb," Tom Taylor added, "but three it will have to stay. That's what I paid for it. You can have it for the same."

The smile left Caleb's face, and he wondered what his father would do in a case like this. He thought of Tom Taylor saying he was like his father. Maybe it was true, he thought. Like him in all ways but one. He was not a quitter. He had the heart of a woods-man. And with luck before the winter was over he would have enough pelts to prove it.

"That's a heap of money," Caleb said.

"Perhaps," Tom Taylor said. "But when I was a boy I would have plowed the top of a mountain for a knife like that."

"I . . . I'd plow a mountain, too," Caleb said, "if there was any need for plowing it."

"I believe you would," Tom Taylor said. "But there ought to be other ways. Let's see . . . you could gather cherry bark. It would take a lot though, so much that gathering it would be almost as hard as plowing a mountain. Ginseng and sassafras won't be good until spring. Course, my being in the store so long has dulled my wits when it comes to the woods. A woodsman would know ways."

Caleb turned from the knife and stared at the traps. "How much did you say the traps would cost?" he asked.

A frown came to Tom Taylor's face. "The traps?" he said, rubbing his chin. "Maybe you would have to plow a mountain to earn the knife and the traps, too. That would be a lot to earn at one time. You stand a good chance to earn one or the other. Both I'm not too sure. I'd still have to have a quarter apiece for the traps. Maybe you ought to think hard about earning the knife."

A frown came to Caleb's face. Tom Taylor reminded him of his father. For some strange reason Caleb had the feeling that Tom Taylor too was against his earning the traps. Perhaps, he thought, the store had dulled Tom's wits.

Caleb became more determined. "I want to earn the traps first," he said. "I can earn the knife with the hides I can catch."

"All right," Tom Taylor said. "A woodsman makes his own decisions. Tell you what . . . if your mind is made up and you can make a payment on the traps I'll hold the others until you catch your furs. I'll hold the knife a while longer too."

Caleb stared around the store. The sewing hoop cost a dollar. With the money left he could buy only four traps. Caleb reached into his pocket. He hesitated, looking again toward the knife.

"Tell you what," Tom Taylor said, "why don't you think about it? You've got two days until Christmas. You can have until Christmas Eve to make the payment on the traps."

The sun had set by the time Caleb reached the cabin and the shadows had come to the valley. The night winds again shook the limbs of the sugar maple.

His mother sat in front of the grate fire, sewing. Her willow hoop was old and uneven and many times his mother had to stop sewing to pull the cloth tight again between the wooden rims where it had slipped. The metal hoop would not allow the cloth to slip. It would be like the brown locust tree that grew along the mountainside, age would never weaken it. The metal hoop would hold the cloth firm and neat.

"Did you see the knife again, Caleb?" his mother asked, not looking up.

"I . . . I seen the traps, too," Caleb said. "And Tom Taylor said if I paid something down on them he'd hold the rest for me until I could catch enough furs to pay for them."

"And would you pay something down on the knife, too?" his mother asked.

"I'll earn the knife with the hides, too," Caleb said.

"The knife is all right, Caleb," his mother said, looking up for the first time. "The traps I'm not sure about. Somehow it doesn't seem right for you to take the muskrats from the creek."

"Pa did," Caleb said. "And Grandpa did, too."

"But your father doesn't take them now," his mother said.

"Pa . . . Pa's a quitter," Caleb said, feeling the tears come to his eyes.

"No," Caleb," his mother said, stretching the cloth again. "Your father is not a quitter. He is a great woodsman, perhaps much greater than he used to be. That is why he no longer traps."

Caleb frowned. He couldn't understand his mother. But, he thought, why should he? She was a woman, and what did a woman know about trapping? His mother was against him, too. Because his father had quit she was asking him to be a quitter, too. If his father had not been a quitter he would have saved his traps for Caleb to use and then he wouldn't have to worry about earning them along with earning the knife. But he had not saved the traps. They weren't at the cabin.

"All woodsmen trap muskrats," Caleb said.

"Maybe," his mother said, looking again from the cloth. "There was a time too when they did more things than trap muskrats. There was a time when I watched your father stand under the maple in the yard and shoot wild turkey. And today the only turkey we see are behind wire fences like chickens. There was a time too when deer came to the creek to drink and their paths honeycombed the hills. The only paths you see today are made by cattle. Muskrat and mink were as thick on the creek as the berry of the elderberry bush. There was no skill needed to catch them. Men of the valley called themselves woodsmen.

Your father was one of them. They shot the wild turkey and deer, killing them all and leaving nothing to build again. They trapped the muskrats. But trapping was slow and only done at night, so it wasn't fast enough. So they traveled the creek during the day to dig them out. The more they caught, the greater woodsmen they thought they were. Funny"— his mother stretched the cloth again—"your grandpa was an old man then. And he talked to your father just as your own father is talking to you now. And then one day something happened. It had something to do with a field of corn, I think. Your father never really told me. But men don't talk men-talk to women. But whatever happened in that field of corn was to make your father a great woodsman. I wished your grandpa had lived to see it. He wouldn't have hurried it up while he was here, though. He allowed your father to make his own decisions. And you will make yours. If you choose and earn the traps they're yours. But either way, Caleb, you have no reason to feel ashamed of your father. He isn't a quitter. Perhaps the day will come when you will see."

Sleep did not come easily to Caleb that night. Perhaps, he told himself, as he listened to the wind against the logs of the cabin, he was just anxious for morning to come so that he could make his down payment on the traps. And yet when he closed his eyes it was not the traps or the knife that he saw. It was the stub-footed muskrat under the log trying to hold the crab apple. And he saw the wild turkey his mother had spoken of. What wonderful thing, he thought, if he could go into the mountains and hunt them. But they were gone, perhaps never to come again. If the hunters had only left a few for seed, he thought. But they had been greedy and taken them all. They had cut down the whole flock. And he became angry with the hunters. He thought of the animals and the birds that lived in the mountains now. There were the quail. But many days they could not be found, for the coveys were small and scattered. He had never seen a wild deer. If you traveled the mountains all day stomping the brush and killed two rabbits you were considered a good woodsman. What would happen, he thought, if he didn't hunt the quail and rabbit or trap the musk-rat for a few seasons? Would they come back strong and tall like the corn had in the strip below the cabin?

And then Caleb shook the thought from his mind. The game was here to be taken. And a man was not a woodsman if he did not take game. If a man was a quitter he was just a quitter, there was really no excuse if he had lost the heart to be a woodsman. And yet his father had told him about the corn. He had told Caleb's mother. His father must have thought Caleb was a man and would understand.

When Caleb woke Christmas Eve had come to the valley. And with it a light sprinkling of snow, cover-ing the ground as white as the clouds above the ridge.

Caleb did not travel to the store early as he had planned, for there was much to be done at the cabin. He gathered wood and brought canned food from the cellar that his mother would fix for Christmas dinner. It was the custom for all the cooking to be done on the day before, so Christmas Day could be a day of rest and peace. And Caleb knew it would also be the day that his father would return from the upper Big Sandy.

It was evening before Caleb turned down the path toward the mouth of the hollow. Along the way he looked again for signs of muskrat. But the snow had come early in the morning covering any tracks that might have been made earlier in the night. He walked fast and before he knew it the store came into sight. And quicker still he was staring at Tom Taylor behind the counter.

"Well, Caleb," Tom Taylor said, "today is the day. All of the traps are the same, seasoned well. How many will you take?"

"Can . . . can you wrap the sewing hoop for me?" Caleb asked.

Tom Taylor pulled a wrapped package from under the counter. Caleb looked toward the glass case. Tom Taylor had put the knife away.

"Wish I could see the look on your mother's face when she opens the package," Tom Taylor said. "Wrapped it real pretty, too. Glad I don't have to wrap the traps."

Caleb stared toward the end of the room. In the corner sat a wooden keg, filled with large red apples.

"How . . . how much are the apples?" he asked.

"Apples?" Tom Taylor said, a frown coming to his face. "Oh, I see. Guess you are a trapper at that. You know that this has been a bad year in the valley for apples. Hardly a tree bore. The ones that did were high on the mountain, too far for a muskrat to travel to gather them for winter storage. When apples are so scarce, they are the best bait a man can use to catch muskrats. Scarcity makes the price higher for us humans too. Reckon I'd have to have sixty cents a dozen."

"How . . . how much?" Caleb asked again.

Tom Taylor laughed. "Fifty cents," he said, "and not a penny less."

"Give me two dozen," Caleb said.

Tom Taylor gathered the apples in a paper sack. He handed the sack to Caleb and took the two dollars.

"That's a lot of apples to use for bait," he said. "Guess your ma will use some to bake pies with."

Caleb turned toward the door.

"Caleb," Tom Taylor said, "you haven't forgotten our bargain. Half down for the traps today. I can't give you any more time. There's another fellow wants the traps if you don't take them."

"I . . . I haven't forgotten," Caleb said, turning out the door.

A short distance up the path Caleb stopped and stared back at the store. Tom Taylor stood in the door, a smile on his face. Caleb turned and started on up the path.

He did not stop again until he had come to the old fallen tree where he had seen the stub-pawed muskrat. Here he knelt and placed several of the red apples under the log, brushing away the snow. And as he walked up the creek he spread the apples along the bank.

Near the cabin he hid the sack and sneaked in the back door, hiding the package from his mother. She would not see it until morning when she came to the grate to rekindle the fire and saw it lying in front of the grate where he would place it during the night.

That night in bed he thought that his mother would never fall asleep as he lay there thinking what she would say when Christmas came and she would find the package. After a long while the cabin became quiet and he sneaked the package in front of the grate. And when he went back to bed and closed his eyes he saw the old stub-footed muskrat crawling from the water and finding the red apples under the log where he had placed them. Those apples would be sweet as honey and they were so large that the old muskrat could eat them from the ground without having to hold them. And for some reason when Caleb thought of the old muskrat, a good feeling came over him. One day, he thought, there would be many muskrats on the creek and he would be able to trap all he wanted. The waiting would be hard. He thought of the field of corn. And he thought too of his grandpa. His grandpa had been proud of his father. Perhaps he was even proud of Caleb. On a night as clear as tonight he would be able to see through the clouds. And then he thought of the knife and tears came to his eyes. He realized now that he had wanted the knife much worse than the traps. But perhaps one day Tom Taylor would have another knife, and with so many muskrats on the creek he would be able to take enough to earn it.

Morning came and Caleb was up before his mother. He sneaked into the room and waited for her to come to the grate. He heard her footsteps. Slowly she walked into the room. She spotted the package and a smile came to her face.

She picked up the package and opened it. Her eyes grew wide as she stared at the hoop.

" 'Pon-my-word," she said. And then something fell to the floor. His mother picked up the package. "Well, Caleb," she said, "this one has your name on it."

Caleb's eyes grew wide as he took the package. His hands trembled as he opened it. He stared at the brown-handled knife.

"It's from your father," she said.

"But . . . but . . ." Caleb could not talk.

"You see, Caleb," his mother said, "before your father left he gathered up his traps and took them to Tom Taylor. He knew you had your eyes set on the knife, so he bargained with Tom Taylor, knowing that you'd see the knife and the traps and that you'd have to make a decision. If, before Christmas, you were to make an effort to get the traps your father would not try to stop you. If you had chosen the traps they would have been yours as a Christmas present. But . . . if you decided against the traps . . . if something had changed your mind . . . the traps were to go as payment for the knife. Your father will be mighty proud of you, Caleb. He'll feel proud to know that his son is such a great woodsman."

Caleb stared at the knife, still not able to talk. Tom Taylor, he thought, had known this all the time. And he had said nothing. He had pretended that the store had dulled his wits.

"What a happy Christmas this is," his mother said. "I have a real metal sewing hoop; you have a fine knife; and your father has been given the one Christmas present he wanted."

Caleb ran his fingers over the handle of the knife. He stared out the window. Before darkness came again to the valley, he knew the greatest woodsman in the whole world would walk the path to the cabin.

7.
The Death of Aunt Lottie

AUNT Lottie lived with her nephew Eff seven miles from the mouth of Birdsong Creek where we lived. To reach her place you traveled the bed of the creek if the weather was dry, or a rugged brier-covered path high on the bank if the creek was up and flowing.

Ma never took us to see Aunt Lottie often. During the last years she lived along the creek, seldom more than once a year. And this was usually on Decoration Day when we went into the hills to gather wild flowers to place over the graves of our dead; to clean the cemetery and build the mounds where the snows of winter had sunk them. Ma claimed that progress had come to the mouth of Birdsong Creek, hills had been cleaned for cattle pasture and lot-selling for houses. Only deep in the hollow did the wild flowers remain untouched and suitable for the dead. And that's why I really came to know and love Aunt Lottie.

Her house was gray-logged, and the grass was always tall in the yard. Nearby, rock cliffs slid into the earth with caves under them, and opossum grapevines hung over the caves like brown eyebrows over deep, dark eyes, and lizards dropped from them like gray tears.

Aunt Lottie was blind, yet long before we reached the yard she would be standing at the edge of the porch waving her arms. Loneliness had made her hearing as keen as a squirrel's.

"Now you stay with your Aunt Lottie, Isaac," Ma would say on this once-a-year trip.

And Aunt Lottie would turn her blind eyes toward the sound of Ma's voice, grin and say to her, "Lord, Ellie, don't you worry about Lottie. You come here to pick flowers for the dead and on this day you think old Lottie needs tending to. What about all the other days of the year when I'm here by myself? You go on to the hills and leave Isaac here with me. Not to tend, but to keep me company for a spell." And then she would sweep her hand in the direction of the yard. "You just mind and don't pick the heads from the flowers in the yard. I love to smell them. I can tell the seasons by smell. Bet the flowers are pretty now that they're in bloom, ain't they, Ellie?"

And this was the one time that I loved to be left behind on a trip. I would much rather have sat here with Aunt Lottie than have gone chasing lizards over the rocks with my sister Lisa and my brother Sim, fooling Ma into thinking they were looking for wild flowers. I loved to sit on the porch and watch Aunt Lottie's long white hair blow in the wind that turned and swept

the edges of the cliffs and brought the smell of the flowers across the yard. And I would look at Aunt Lottie and say:

"What flower smell does the wind bring, Aunt Lottie?"

"Honeysuckle," she'd answer. "See the vines near the cliffs?" The smell *would* be honeysuckle and the vines sure enough *were* near the cliffs.

"What does the wind bring now?" I would ask.

"Wild daisies from right here in the yard," she said.

I judged Aunt Lottie to be the smartest person along the creek, and I told her so.

She reared back in her split-bottomed chair and said, "Now let me just see about that." She brushed her long white hair. "What grade of school are you in now, Isaac?"

"Fourth," I said.

"Reckon you got me beat then," she said. And she placed her hand on her forehead as if she were studying. "Not really bad, though. Just got me beat by . . . let's see . . . about four years, I'd say." And she laughed into the wind.

I also judged that Aunt Lottie could see better with her blind eyes than most people could with seeing eyes. Ma and my brother and sister would hardly be out of sight before Aunt Lottie would walk into the cabin and come back with her dulcimer under her arm and her feather-quill pick between her lips. She would sit down in the chair and pull the dulcimer to her lap and I'd sit waiting and watching for her long white hair to get caught in the strings of the dulcimer, although her hair never did. She would strum and sing and her eyes would quiver and she'd say, "Lordy, what company this dulcimer is to your Aunt Lottie."

"But how do you know where to put your fingers, Aunt Lottie?" I'd ask, looking into the nothingness of her eyes.

"Good Lord just put a little music inside me to help keep away this powerful loneliness," she said. "It comes from the heart, runs down the arm, and comes dripping off the ends of my fingers." And to show me she'd strum fast and furious and sing:

"Give me the flowers while I live,
    Trying to cheer me on;
Useless are flowers that you give
    After the soul is gone."

Once, while Aunt Lottie was playing this song, I sneaked away to the yard and clipped a handful of wild daisies and brought them to her. She took the flowers and I saw her eyelids quiver. A tear came from one eye. It scared me at first, because I didn't know that a blind person could cry; I thought that Aunt Lottie's eyes were sealed so that nothing could come from them. And then Aunt Lottie hugged the dulcimer closer to her and strummed with the quill again:

"Sweet bunch of daisies
Picked from the dell
Whisper you love me,
Daisies won't tell."

I felt my legs quiver. I wanted more than anything to throw my arms around Aunt Lottie's neck and tell her that I loved her very much, but I was ashamed to. Ma had always told us that Aunt Lottie deeply resented any show of pity because of her blindness and I was afraid that she might mistake love for pity. So I looked at the flowers and the grayness of her hair and the wrinkles of her skin. She reached out and touched me, her fingers moving over my skin like they had over the strings of the dulcimer. She said:

"I can't see you, Isaac, but there is music in you, too. I hear you pat-pat your feet on the boards of the porch, and I'm glad. For one day when you know the awfulness of the loneliness of the hills you'll be able to whip it with your music. When I die I want you to have my dulcimer. Here, you must learn to play it now."

It made me sad to hear Aunt Lottie speak of dying. And Aunt Lottie must have known this, for she belittled death on her face and said:

"You can't see a song, Isaac. But you know it's there because you can feel it. My death will be akin to a song. You'll find me in the strings of the dulcimer."

I was seven years of schooling ahead of Aunt Lottie the summer she died. Cousin Eff sent a neighbor to tell us. Heavy rains had been in the hills, and the creek was muddy and swift. We walked the muddy path high on the bank, and Ma made us walk in front so if we slipped and fell in the creek she could catch us as we went by.

The damp earth had made the grass in the yard

grow taller, and the wind had come of the night to
break it over and mat it until you could hardly walk
to the porch. Aunt Lottie was in a pine coffin that Eff
had made. She looked like she had lain down to sleep
for a while. Her long white hair had been combed to
her side and her eyes were closed.

"Glad you got here," Eff said, walking to meet us.
"Lottie's been dead three days now. Don't believe I
could have kept her aboveground another night. I
couldn't make it up the slope with her by myself." He
looked off toward the coffin. "Lottie never wanted to
be buried in the low ground. Picked her a place long
ago up that knoll where the big pine tree stands." His
lips quivered. "Had to send a neighbor; didn't want
to leave Lottie here alone."

And I thought that if Aunt Lottie could have heard
she would have quarreled at Eff for inferring that she
needed tending to. I looked off toward the pine tree. I
remembered the many times that Aunt Lottie had
talked about the lone pine on the ridge above the
house. Below the pine a small strip of land had been
cleared for a garden, and while Eff worked the strip,
he used to lead Aunt Lottie up the hill and let her sit
under the shade of the pine. High up where the wind
blew, and through the needles of the great pine it sang
a mournful song.

Aunt Lottie had not been born blind. Age had
closed her eyes slowly and shadows and images had
remained in front of them for a long time. And the
image of the great pine standing alone on the ridge

with nothing but the sky behind it had been the last to disappear. So there was a closeness between her and the tree and she had asked about it often.

"Is it still there?" she would ask. "Is it still there?" And she would sit on the porch looking toward the tree, never once forgetting the direction it stood.

Being so near the small garden patch, the pine tree had long become a sentry post for the crows that came to eat Eff's corn. Aunt Lottie knew and remembered this before I was old enough to visit. It had become a ritual with her. And often, after I was old enough to count, she would sit on the porch staring toward the pine and say:

"How many crows are in the pine tree?"

"One . . . two . . . three . . ." and then other crows would circle and light in the pine and mix me up.

Aunt Lottie would know that the crows were circling the tree and mixing me up and she would grin and say:

"I reckon the crows are sitting around the top of the pine like petals around the center of a daisy, ain't they?"

"Yes," I would answer

"Coming and going, ain't they?"

"Yes."

"Not much use to try and count, then," she'd say.

And she would laugh to the wind and point toward the pine. She'd say:

"Look toward the center of the pine. Now there's a big black crow sitting there watching old Eff. If Eff tries to sneak up the slope, that crow will warn the other crows that Eff is coming. My, I could save that old crow a lot of sitting if I was able to tell him how crooked Eff is with a gun. He wouldn't have to watch sentry at all. He could swoop down there and eat with the rest of the crows."

"But won't he get to eat?" I would say, feeling sorry for the lone crow.

"Yes," Aunt Lottie said. "Soon, a crow will swing out of Eff's corn patch and rest him for a spell. Now, if I was a crow I'd rather sit in the top of that big pine than eat anytime. I could find myself something better to look for than Eff." And she laughed. She hummed:

> "Neath the pine, neath the pine,
> Where the sun will never shine,
> Winds whisper and the cold winds blow."

A neighbor helped us carry the coffin up the slope. We buried her there like a sentry crow overlooking the land below. That evening as we walked down the creek toward the mouth an awful loneliness I had never known came over me. And I thought of Aunt Lottie's dulcimer and what she had said. I begged Ma to let me go back to the cabin and get the dulcimer. It had been promised to me. The loneliness had come. and I would need it. Ma said:

"Hush, child it's a bad omen to take the belongings of the dead before the sun has set over their graves."

The sun rose and set many times. Kin and no kin. neither bothering to ever come and sit and be company to Aunt Lottie, came whenever they caught Eff gone from the cabin, to plunder her belongings. I was

afraid they had taken the dulcimer. And when I cried
Ma said:

"Hush, child, it's a far worse omen to take from the
dead what you have not been welcomed to in life."

During the days that followed, I hoped Ma was
right. And I hoped that if they had taken the dulcimer
there would be no music in it; that the music had been
sealed forever in the fingers of Aunt Lottie.

And then one evening, a month after Aunt Lottie's
death, Eff came to our house carrying the worn dulcimer case under his arm. He handed me the case, and
before he went off to talk with Ma he said:

"The dulcimer belongs to you, Isaac. Lottie told me
so on her deathbed. I hid it under a board of the floor
until I had time to bring it."

I sat down under the tree in the yard and opened
the dulcimer case. The dulcimer was there, the picking quill laced between the strings. And the bunch of
daisies that I had once gathered for Aunt Lottie was
inside the case, too, their smell and color stolen by
time.

I took the quill and pulled it softly over the strings.
And Aunt Lottie was there.

8.
Hospitality

I had hired on the side-wheeler *Nellie Ren* at Pittsburgh as an extra hand, making an agreement with the side-wheeler's captain, Arsh Grey, to work my board and passage to New Orleans. The *Nellie Ren* had not been a matter of choice for me; it had, in fact, been the only boat that would take me, my owing it all (so I was told by the wharf hounds along the dock) to Captain Arsh's mellowing in his many years along the river to the point of picking up strays. I wasn't broke. I had worked out a little money loading coal in Pittsburgh. I carried all of it in my pocket when I boarded the *Nellie Ren* except a fin which I stuck in my shoe for hard times or fool-thinking. And that's how I ended up in Sourwood, a half-mountain, half-water town hedged up on the Kentucky shore of the big Ohio like a footlog to a big bald mountain named Sourwood.

It was late of the evening when Captain Arsh pulled the *Nellie Ren* to shore to lay off some items he had brought from Pittsburgh. And he'd take shore leave

since many of his old friends still lived in Sourwood
which, as he told it, had once been the roughest, rowdiest, and richest little town along the river. Once a main
stop for all boats, only the *Nellie Ren* still paused here
now. This, too, was attributed by members of the crew
to Captain Arsh's mellowing. To me Sourwood looked
as naked as the shadow of the mountain that
stretched out over the river as far as the channel. But
with time on my hands I thought I would give it a look
and steady my legs to land.

I got no farther than the Sourwood Bar, being ac-
companied there by Captain Arsh and introduced by a
wink to the bartender. The rest remained as misty as
a fog along an early morning river. A few drinks. A
few more. And I woke up along the riverbank, the
sand flies pestering, the sun in my face and the *Nellie
Ren* nowhere in sight. I was sick, rolled, broke, and
New Orleans a long way off.

I looked toward my feet, saw that my shoes were
still on, and figured the fin was still with me. I stumbled
my way into the Sourwood Bar and ordered a drink.
The bartender poured and held the glass on the bar.

"I been rolled," I said, shaking my head and frowning from pain.

"They all have," he said, pulling the glass nearer
him.

I placed the palm of my hand over the top of the
glass.

"Leave it be," I said. "I been rolled, but I got
enough left to pay for the drink."

"They all say that, too," he said, reaching his free

hand toward the wooden mall on the shelf behind him big enough to knock a bull's head off with. And his reaching it without turning was proof that he probably would and had done just that. "You try your other hand. Reach easy and when you spread it out hope that you got something in it besides air. I ain't a man for pouring back in the bottle. Nerves ain't too steady."

I kept my eyes on him, lifted my leg, jerked off my shoe, and came up with the five-dollar bill.

"What sort of town is this anyway?" I said.

"Hospitable," he said. "Hospitable and cautious."

"And thirty bucks richer," I said.

"Where you from?" he asked.

"Upriver."

"Where you heading?"

"Downriver."

"Hope to get far on what you got left?" he said.

"Fill the glass," I said, shoving it to him. "Nope. I worked a lousy two months in Pittsburgh for that money. I'm still spitting coal dust. Now I got to grub it all over again. Any work around here?"

"You kidding," he said. "If you lost money in this town last night it's fifty per cent richer than what you found it."

I gauged the morning sun coming through the window.

"Well," I said, "I been in this damn town too long. I know that!"

"Hate to see you leave mad," he said.

"I ain't mad," I said. "I'm just sick." I placed the glass on the bar and turned to go.

"Wait," he said, looking toward the door.

I turned and saw the little man walk in. Small, beady-eyed, and a hump on his back the size of a bedroll.

"Morning, Eff," the bartender said.

"Evening, Tom," he answered, tipping his hat, yellow dust scattering from it. "All right if I have a beer?"

The bartender looked at me, frowned, and looked back at the little man.

"Now, Eff, you know I ain't for getting into trouble with Quildy."

"It's all right, Tom," he said. "She ain't home yet."

The bartender slid a mug out to him and stopped me just as I had turned again to go.

"Wait, stranger," he said. "I just might be able to help you." He looked quickly at the small man. "Still working on the new cabin, Eff? I mean you ain't finished and . . ."

Eff gurgled through a mouthful of beer. "Nope. Should have. But that drifter you sent me two weeks ago left after the second day. Can't find a man willing to work nowdays."

"You working today?" the bartender asked, glancing toward me.

"Was," Eff said. "Got started early, but the rain come and got the best of me. Thought I'd come in for a beer and let it slack. Mighty lonesome up there without Quildy."

Well, the sun had been long playing through the windows of the saloon. But I didn't give the talk of rain much thought. I didn't know where he lived, how far. Summer rains were odd. One man's yard could wash away while his neighbor's baked in drought.

"Could you use an extra hand up there?" the bartender asked.

"Might if he could work," Eff said, looking at me for the first time.

"Now wait a minute," I said.

"You want work or was you just yapping like all the others?" the bartender said. "You stagger in here claiming you got rolled in this town, asking about work to get on. Mighty unhospitable. Me willing to go to bat for a total stranger. You trying to fool someone, mister?"

I glanced at the mall and said, "I'll take the job. I'll stay a week."

"Two dollars a day and board if you work good." Eff grinning with his mouth open enough for me to see the foam of the beer around his rotted teeth.

"Good enough for me," I said.

"I'm obliged to you again, Tom," the little man said to the bartender, tipping his hat. "Don't know what I'd done up till now if it wasn't for you and Capt'n Arsh. Ain't always got a lot of work, but it sure helps whip the loneliness." He looked at me. "Well, if you're ready, young feller, I'll help you carry your belongings."

The mentioning of Captain Arsh crossed my mind at the time, also remembering the wink of the introduction. But my thoughts were vague. What I saw now was a chance of getting out of Sourwood, and I was full of gratefulness.

"I'm ready," I said to Eff. "I'm wearing all the belongings I got." I nodded to the bartender. "Listen, this town, I mean what I said . . ."

"Skip it," the big bartender said. "It's a hospitable little town, Sourwood. Try to treat strangers right."

It must have been more than five miles to where the old man lived. Dirt road all the way. Dusty. We crossed over to the back of town and kept along the foothills and then turned up a hollow a mile or so and then off a spur branch for a fair quarter mile. Deep in one of the wrinkles of the big mountain; raw and lonesome with the stillness of a night river.

There were two cabins: one old and gray and so shadowed by trees that dampness grew it heavy with moss. The old man stood in the yard, his denim pants weather-worn and time-whitened as his hair, and his faded shirt took up by the hump on his back until it stuck out of his pants. He pointed his crooked finger toward the new cabin that he was building less than two hundred feet from the old one. A little farther out of the shade so that the sun fell across the half-finished roof, eye-blinding against the white oak shingles. The foundation stood on neatly chiseled stones carried from the mountain, I supposed, and chipped to form, I was sure, in the yard since the chips were placed in small piles of rocks.

"Kinda trashy right now," he said. "But won't be when Quildy—that's my woman—comes home. She'll use them chips to wall off a flower garden. She always planned to do that. Well, make yourself to home. We'll bunk in the old cabin if you don't mind. I promised

Quildy when the new cabin was finished she'd be the first to sleep in it."

"That's all right with me," I said. "Where do I start earning my money?"

"Hewing logs," he said, pointing. "Hewing logs."

I guess I wasn't very sociable that first day. I mean here I was near broke and New Orleans so far downriver. I kept my eyes on the logs and the chips flew. I stopped only now and then to wipe away the sweat and to take a drink of water the old man brought and offered me in a gourd. And I watched him walk away, the big hump on his back jerking up and down as if it had a life of its own, trying to break loose from his back and make the most of it. I watched him scoot to the roof like an old lizard, sit himself on it and nail at the shingles.

He fixed supper that night and brought it to the small room he had given me near the backside of the old cabin. He sat down in a chair, frowned and wrung his hands.

"I hope we can get the cabin livable this week and be a little ahead of the snow," he said.

"Snow?" I said. "It's July."

"That's right," he said, more as an exclamation than a question. "Man loses all track of time in the mountains. But you can't tell about the weather, though." He stood up and turned. "I'm obliged to you. I mean the way you worked today. Mighty hard. Lonesome tonight, ain't it?"

"I guess so," I answered, watching him work the hump through the door.

The old man woke me at daylight. He was holding breakfast out to me. He sat down in the chair, leaning over as if to rest his back from the burden of the great hump. The morning wind seeped through the cracks of the wall logs and the old man stunk so bad I could hardly eat.

"I guess I overslept," I said, seeing a streak of sun play across the floor.

"That's all right," he said. "I like to see folks sleep good. Quildy's that way."

At noon the old man asked me:

"You think this kitchen ought to be over here, or should I make this a bedroom? I mean if the kitchen goes here, then I ought to spread the room out some. Quildy always wanted a big kitchen."

I had worked all morning with my head full of thoughts, most of them New Orleans, and my lips were dry thinking of cold beer.

"Look, old man," I said. "I don't know nothing about houses. Why don't you ask your wife? It's her home. She's got to live in it, not me."

"Oh, I wouldn't want to do that," he said. "I want most of the big worries out of the way when she comes. She's had her share of worries." He frowned and the hump on his back shook. "I'm sorry I made you mad. I ain't too smart. Want to take time out to eat supper? I'll sit over here if you want."

"Look," I said, and my eyes crossed his weathered hands, broken and bleeding wherever he had missed one of the shingles. "It ain't supper. It's dinner."

"Well, it's just eating," he said. "Just eating." He turned to walk away.

"Listen, old man," I said, "I ain't mad at nobody but myself. Let's eat together."

"I'm glad," he said. "It's powerful lonesome eating alone."

We sat down to eat.

"You married?" he asked.

"Nope."

"Then you wouldn't know," he said, staring off into the mountain. "You wouldn't know how lonesome a place can get."

"Well," I said, "it it's that bad, why don't you go and bring your woman home now? I mean I don't mind sleeping in the woodshed until the cabin's ready. It'll beat a riverbank all to blazes."

"I couldn't do that," he said. "I mean me and Quildy made it up she'd come home when the work was done. She's not to drive a nail, lift a board, or turn her hand. She's had her share of work. And I aim to make it all up to her. She ain't ever going to have to work again."

"How long you been on the new cabin?" I asked.

"Don't recollect exactly," he said, squinting his eyes and turning his lips to figure. "One, two, seven years. I don't know. Long, lonesome time."

"And you been apart all this time?" I asked.

"Yep," he said, smiling. "Just the way we planned it. Took her over to stay with neighbors the day I started building."

"Well," I said, "you do go to see her?"

"That's the only thing that keeps me going," he said.

"She must be a mighty fine woman to be that patient," I said.

"Quildy is a fine woman," he said. "I mean we lived here in this old cabin fifty maybe sixty years. I don't know numbers. Taking in washing. Carrying baskets of clothes up and down the hollow. Rubbing, scrubbing. Hands red and sometimes bleeding. Me sometimes on the hot hillsides trying to grub land too poor to grow weeds. Sometimes in town drinking and fooling around a little too. I mean they ain't no need my lying about it. But it's over now. My drinking to the point of fooling around and her waiting here lonesome."

"Well, I'm glad," I said. "The cabin ought to be in shape to bring her home this weekend."

"If the snow will just stay off," he said, taking the dirty dishes to the cabin.

The day was long, and I was tired. I had been tasting a cold beer all day. And so when dark came I splashed my face with water and turned out the door. When I reached the edge of the yard the old man came running, sideways to keep the hump on his back from knocking him off balance.

"You ain't leaving me?" he said, a starving look in his eyes. "I mean I ain't done or said nothing wrong to you, have I?"

"No," I said. "Everything's just fine, old man. I'm just going for a beer. I'll be coming back. Can I bring you a cold one?"

"No," he said. "I never drink no more after sundown. A promise to Quildy."

"See you later then," I said. "Don't wait up. I'll be in bed come daylight."

"I'm obliged to you for that," the old man said.

I walked into the Sourwood Bar dry enough to soak up a beer from the distance of the door.

He looked off toward the mountain.

"Listen, stranger," the bartender said when I reached the bar, "now about that job . . ."

"Give me a beer," I said, not in a talking mood. "I'm doing my share of the work."

A grin crossed his face.

"No hard feelings?" he said.

"Why should there be?" I answered. "I got three more lousy days to go and then I'll be out of this hole."

"Still working, eh?" he said. He leaned over the bard and squinted at several men gathered around a poker table.

"A week," I said. "That's all I promised. A week is five days to me. Saturday is gone, and Sunday I sleep it off."

Eff ain't brought his woman home yet, eh?" he said as if talking more to the men at the poker table than to me.

"Friday," I said. "He'll bring her home then." I laid out the money for the drink.

"This one is on the house," he said.

"What do I mark it up to?" I said.

"Hospitality," he said. "Hospitality." He grinned.

The old man was really getting to me. I mean snow

in July, supper at dinner, and dinner at breakfast. And
Quildy. I mean I never was much to listening to man-
talk about a woman unless the talker was me and the
woman was mine. Several times I wanted to give it all
up, just walk off, no pay, no nothing. Just off. Away.
But I couldn't. I kept seeing that big hump on his
back, jerking, pulling at his strength like a leech. I
even got to thinking at times how lucky he was. A
livable cabin. Roots. Even if the roots were deep in
this godforsaken Sourwood Mountain. A woman willing to bear it all out and then come back for more of
the same. The only woman I had ever known came
back for more drinks and a double chance to roll me.

Friday I looked at the old man and then at the
cabin. Somehow feeling a part of it, glad that it was
over for me and yet glad that I had been a part of it.
I mean a river tramp like me don't get many chances
to do much good along the way. I said:

"Well, old man, I guess this is it. I'll take my pay
and be off your land."

The old man kicked at a doodle of stone chips, his
head down. Then he looked over the mountain. Shadows were streaking through the trees and it would
soon be dark.

"I hope you won't get mad," he said.

"What for?" I asked.

"Well," he said, "I never been very trustful when it
comes to money. Oh, don't get me wrong. I ain't a
man to cheat or not pay. It's just that when it comes
to over a dollar, Quildy always handles it."

I should have been mad, I guess. But I never had been much at handling money myself. I said:

"OK. So you want me to wait until you get her. I mean it won't take long?"

"No," he said. "It ain't a long distance. Cross the mountain a ways." He turned. "You could come if you want. I mean it's lonesome to walk alone, and it's lonesome to stay alone."

Well, I guessed walking the mountains carrying a hump on your back did make it tough. Alone. Maybe I could help him the rest of the way. I could get my money just as easy from there as here, sleep the night along the river and chance catching a boat.

"All right," I said. "Let's go."

The old man didn't talk much. Breathed hard up the side of the mountain, stopping here and there to shift the hump. On top the ridge he turned into scrub oaks and saw briers.

"How could anyone live in this hell-forsaken country?" I said, picking my way through the briers. "We got much farther to go?"

"Country grows over you," the old man said. "Country grows over you and holds you like a vine. Almost there now."

He turned toward the point of a knuckle-shaped bluff. I stopped to wipe away the sweat and take a brier from my arm. I caught up just as the last of the sun was settling over the small cemetery. The old man was on his knees, bowed as if the hump would pull him across the mound of earth in front of him.

"Quildy," he whispered. "Quildy, it's Eff. Come to take you home."

I left the old man there. I didn't know how far downriver it was to the next town. Or if it would be as hospitable as Sourwood. I could have a long way to travel.

9.
The Used-to-Be Dog

THE old man lived in a one-room shack perched up on the side of a hill along Blackjack Creek, and he owned a little straddle-legged dog that he claimed was a cross between a feist and a ferret, making it half dog and half varmint.

It was the summer that the coal mine played out over at Harlan, and Pa had moved us to Blackjack where a new one had opened. It was lonely country, and Pa said that I might be keeping my eyes open for a dog of my own to temper the loneliness a bit. That's how come I got tied up with the old man and his Tweedle dog.

I had to pass his place on the mornings Ma sent me to the store at the mouth of the creek.

The old man was always on the porch catching the early morning sun, and one morning he waved me up. It was then that I saw the Tweedle dog. She was stretched out near his feet.

"You be going to the store?" he asked.

"Yes," I said, staring at the dog and thinking I had never seen the likes.

"Be too much trouble for you to fetch me back a twist of tobacco?" he asked.

"No," I answered, "no trouble to fetch."

The little dog wasn't much to look at, but I was dog hungry and her teats were heavy, showing a sign that she was sucking pups. And she was the only dog I had seen since we had moved to Blackjack. I gave her another looking over and said:

"What sort of dog is she?"

"You know dogs?" the old man asked.

"Some," I answered.

"Then you ought to be knowing," he said, "that to begin with they's three sorts of dogs: good dogs, better dogs, and this here Tweedle dog. Tweedle is a cross betwixt a feist and a ferret, making her half dog and half varmint."

She still didn't look like much, but she sounded like something and so I said:

"She sure is bowlegged."

"Got that way from straddling trees," the old man said. "Used to clamp right onto a tree, shinny up, point a possum, coon, or squirrel in the top like a bird dog on quail. Used to be the best in the hills. I spent years looking for a good-sized ferret to cross her to, just about give it all up until I come across one this year. Got me a litter of pups that's prize-winning."

Not wanting to overtalk my welcome, I headed down the hollow thinking about the bowlegs on that little dog. But, mixed in with the redbirds, catbirds, and blue jays I was scaring up among the beech trees that lined the hollow, I saw the litter of pups the old man had spoken of. And as I brushed the morning spider webs out of the path, I kept trying to pick a pup from the litter that didn't have legs like barrel staves, one that might not bring a grin from Pa and a snigger from Ma. I got to thinking that the size of the Tweedle dog was a favor on my side. Her pups would be apt to stay small—small enough to sneak in the house of nights, past Ma, and snuggle up in bed with me, driving away the weird sounds of the wind and the loneliness of the hills. It was then that I got to thinking about something the old man had said: the Tweedle dog *used to be*.

I worried about it terrible, and when I reached the old man's shack and handed him his twist of tobacco I said:

"What do you mean the Tweedle dog used to be?"

"Well, course you wouldn't know, being new here on Blackjack," he said. "But it had something to do with a fox and the worst winter we ever had. The snow came for days and made a ghost of the hills. The long, black fingers of the trees stuck through the deep snow, and the wind played a mournful tune through them." The old man pinched a cud from the twist of tobacco and stuck it in his jaw. He looked down and squinted at the Tweedle dog. He took a deep breath and reared back in his chair.

"The old fox's name was Paddlefoot and he denned over at the rock cliff on Suttler's Mountain. Meanest and biggest fox to ever come to these hills. Stole so many chickens hereabouts that you couldn't get within ten feet of his den without picking your way through the bones. Brazen and didn't try to hide his den at all. You got to have respect for a varmint like that. I guess people wondered why I didn't take the Tweedle dog and roust that fox out, being I was the varmint hunter hereabouts and Tweedle far ahead of anything that had four legs. But, truth is, the many times I had come upon the track of that fox they always led away from my place. I guess he had respect for me same as I had for him. He had stayed away from me and I had stayed away from him. And I had to think about the Tweedle dog, too. I mean she was young as dogs go, and that fox was twice the size of an ordinary fox, twice as mean, and had the whipping of more than one dog to his credit. And the thing about Tweedle was, when you sicked her to trail she held like glue. And where the other dogs could be choked off at the den hole, Tweedle, being half ferret, could go right in and make it a fight to the finish. I just didn't know if Tweedle had had enough experience to tackle old Paddlefoot. I figured the time would have to come later when the two of them would meet.

"Well, like I say, the fox wasn't taking my chickens anyway. But I guess I ought to have known he was too ornery to stay that way. I guess it was a mixture of snow and the reputation of the Tweedle dog that drove the fox on. For he had took to stealing chickens wherever there was the best and meanest dogs around. Making a mockery of the lot of them.

"Trouble first came the night I was over on John's

Creek to a square dance. Down the hill he came, and jerked a pot-size hen from my chicken roost. We saw his tracks, me and Tweedle. And they looked as big as a bear's with the moon shadowing them and all. Well, Tweedle wanted to settle the score that night. Pouted around like she was to blame and all. But I coaxed her off to bide time.

"Now I knew that fox had my chicken and a full stomach. I knew, too, that he had an eyeful of the other fat hens on my roost. And the next day the wind shook snow over the hills again and the flakes were as big as leaves. It looked like more bad weather was coming for sure, and I figured old Paddlefoot would be on the prowl again come dark. He'd be wanting to fatten up before he denned for a few days to wait out the weather. I figured he had my hens in mind to take up the slack in his belly.

"I tried to pacify Tweedle, but it didn't work, and so I went to bed that night listening to the wind howl, and Tweedle took watch inside the henhouse. And sure enough, along toward morning, that old varmint of a fox come sneaking down the mountain back of my house. He crossed over to the henhouse and reached up on the roost for a fat hen. But Tweedle was perched up there on the roost like a chicken and she set her teeth in the fox. The yelp woke me up, and the fight was on. I stepped out into the grayness of the morning just in time to see Tweedle astraddle that fox's back. Clamped to him like she would clamp to the side of a tree. The fox was bucking like a steer and Tweedle was holding like a vise. And up the side of the mountain they went. The land got so steep that they were almost standing straight up and down. I guess the snow made the back of the fox slick, because Tweedle finally slid off. And the long-legged fox hopped in and out of the snow like a jackrabbit. The snow had laid in drifts and Tweedle's legs were so short that her jumps just wouldn't bring her above it. I grabbed me a two-pound can of carbide and took after them. I never saw the Tweedle dog again until I got to the fox's den, but I was able to follow her every step of the way. For she was traveling under the heavy snow, heaving up ridges of snow as she went, traveling like a ground mole. At the mouth of the den she dug to the surface, popped her head out, and with the snow laying around her like a collar, looked at me.

"Well, if that don't beat all, I thought. That fox has sure enough moved in next to me for a showdown. He had left his den in the rocks over on Suttler's Mountain, dug him a shallow home right up on the mountain above my house, intending to clean me out. That took gall. Well, I thought, if it's a fight you want, it's a fight you'll get. First off, I figured this fox would be too smart to have only one entrance to his den. So, I set about to find the other one—the one he would use to come out of when he got in trouble. Sure enough I found it. His getaway hole pushed up next to the roots of an old oak tree, less than ten feet away from the entrance he used to go in and fool you. A little humped knoll separated the two. Well, if my plan was to work I had to keep the fox from sneaking out on me, so I looked at Tweedle and said, 'You stay here and watch this hole, and I'll go around to the entrance and settle with this chicken-stealing varmint.'

"Tweedle squatted there in the snow with her head tilted, looking down toward the hole like the picture of the dog looking down in the morning-glory horn on a Victor phonograph record. Just daring that old fox to come out. Well, I could have let Tweedle go in after him. But I wouldn't. I was still worried about her being able to handle him in a death struggle. That's why I figured to trick Tweedle and settle it my way.

"Once back at the entrance hole, I pulled the can of carbide from my shirt, scooped me out a pocket of earth back in the hole, and poured the carbide in it. I tossed a couple of handfuls of snow over the carbide, and it started to fizzle. The white fumes from it curled, and the wind carried them back into the hole. Soon I heard the fox growling and fussing inside the dark tunnel, and I knew the fumes had reached him. Now, I thought, I'll strike me a match, throw it into the fumes, and blow that fox to kingdomcome. I struck the match, yelled at Tweedle to get ready, and tossed the match onto the carbide just as Tweedle disappeared into the hole she was watching. I guess she mistook me to say 'get him,' instead of 'get ready.'

"Well, the carbide went off, and it blew a hole in the side of the mountain big enough to bury a man in. Knocked me over and bruised me up. I got to my feet and looked around. I couldn't see hide or hair of either the fox or that Tweedle dog. My goodness, I thought, I've done blowed poor Tweedle and that fox into something that didn't even leave a spot or a piece of hair.

"Well, I went back down the mountain feeling low-down and missing poor Tweedle something awful. I was just up to figuring that my varmint-hunting days were over when I reached the porch. And there she was: Tweedle sitting on the porch, trembling and smelling of carbide. A few feet from the porch I saw a big hole in the snow and the ridged-up mound leading to the porch where Tweedle was. Good gosh, I thought, could it be I've blowed poor Tweedle from the mountain high as a blackbird, and she landed here where the hole in the snow is and tunneled her way to the porch? I was so happy that she was alive I picked her up to make over her. But once off the ground she whimpered something awful and I had to set her down.

"That's when I started noticing little things about that dog. I mean she'd still clamp on to a tree all right, but after about two feet up she'd whimper and fall back to her all fours.,Even got to where I had to set her off the porch. She wouldn't go near the edge of it.

"It got to worrying me so bad that I took poor Tweedle into Sourwood one day to see a doctor. We sat there, me and the doctor and Tweedle, and I told the doctor all I knew about it. Well, that doctor shook his head, studied, then walked over and picked Tweedle up. She whimpered, and the Doc set her down.

" 'Just as I figured,' he said, shaking his head and looking at the little dog.

" 'Is it bad, Doc?' I asked, fearing the worst.

" 'That dog has got a case of acrophobia,' " he said. 'Worse case I ever saw on a dog.'

" 'A word that big has got to mean something bad, Doc,' I said. 'Could you break it down some for me?'

"Well," the Doc said, "that dog has done gone higher than she ever intended to go or was put here to go, and she ain't got no intentions of ever going there again. She is feared of height. She caught it from the carbide, and wherever that fox is, he's got it, too. Keep that little dog as low to the ground as you can, give her a few aspirins each day and bring her back once a week for examinations."

The old man broke off another piece of twist, wollered it in his jaw and grinned. "That's what I mean by *used to be*," he said.

The Tweedle dog looked up at him and wagged her tail. The old man patted her on top of her head and looked back at me.

"But you ain't too interested in the big dog," he said. "Being a dogman, I can see it in your eyes. It's the pups you'd be wanting to see."

The old man raised from his chair, moved toward the back of the shack, and motioned for me to follow. The Tweedle dog danced at his feet, whimpering and wagging her tail. I swallowed and followed.

We stopped at a rain barrel that had been turned on its side to make a home. The pups, winding their mother and dinner, tumbled out of the barrel and stumbled toward the Tweedle dog. Four of them! The old man grabbed one on the run—the bowleggedest one of the lot—and handed it to me.

"To fight the loneliness with," he said, and then added, "if you're sure your ma won't skin me out."

"It's all right," I said, wishing I could shout. "Ma says I can have a dog."

As I ran from the yard toward home I could hear the old man laughing into the wind. And once out of sight, I stopped to catch my wind and look again at my dog. I held it in my hand like a piece of firewood and it felt soft and wanting. And then it looked down at the ground and clamped its bowlegs around my arm as if they were vines. I hurried up the path. It don't matter none, I thought. I wouldn't want you to go high, anyway. You might climb a tree, and I couldn't reach you. I'd rather have you under the bed of the nights, fooling Ma and keeping me company.

10.

Froggie Goes A-Courtin'

IF Mark Tarpin could have chosen the man he would have liked to be it would have been Saul Stratton, rather than his father, who was sheriff of the small mountain town of Catlettsville. Saul's home was a shantyboat at the mouth of the Big Sandy River in eastern Kentucky where she empties into the broad Ohio. Up the bank, overlooking the two rivers, stood Catlettsville. Actually, the shantyboat was in the broad Ohio waters, but the Big Sandy carried its own color for a fair piece along the Ohio bank, and as long as the color could be seen by the naked eye, the waters were said to be Big Sandy.

Saul had been born on the shantyboat and it had been his only home. In his many years on the river he had become as close to the water as the cotton-bloom willow. He had his living from the river. In the winter came the muskrat. The summer brought catfish, perch, turtle, and willow limbs full of sap that he could bend and weave into willow chairs.

If Mark could have chosen the season he liked best in the year, it would have been the warm days of summer. This was the time of year that he and the other small boys of the town came down the mudbanks and gathered around the old man on the shantyboat like schools of spring minnows. From the old man, Mark and the boys learned the best fishing holes and the right bait to use. They learned the swimming holes with a sand instead of mud bottom. Blue river mud would stick to your body like scales to a fish, a sure sign that the boys had sneaked a swim.

But most of all when the sun had sifted low among the willows, they loved to sit on the old man's boat and listen to his many strange tales of the river. And when the evening shadows moved over the blue water, the boys gathered close and listened for the low bellow of the great brown river frog to drift over the water. At the first sound of the frog the old man would frown his face, bend his ear upriver, curl his lip and send a croak back upriver to the brush bile where the frog was sitting. Another croak would drift back to the boat, and the old man would smile and shake his head. But before he croaked again he would cup his hand by the side of his mouth and whisper to the boys what the frog had said. For Saul claimed to know frog language and could tell every word said. He said that because of his many years on the river the frogs had permitted him to learn their language. It would be no trouble for him to coax a frog from the brush pile, downriver to the boat, and have it leap from the water to the bow of the boat and even into a burlap sack.

Once Mark had asked to see this miracle, and Saul had looked at him and the other boys and had said:

"Now, Mark, if'n I were to do that, coax the frog here for you boys to see, why this here frog would come to the boat and see all of you and know that I was telling his secret that he had confided in me to keep. He'd go and tell the other frogs, and they might forever leave the river. Then, after you and the boys had gone up the bank, the river would be a mighty lonely place. The winds would settle among the willow grove and quit their fussin', and the river would stretch out and soak up the moon, and I wouldn't have no one to talk to."

There was no doubt that the strange tale of the frog had made an impression on the boys. Especially on Mark, who was always the last to leave the shantyboat, sitting with his eyes fixed on the old man until it became dark and Saul would walk with him to the top of the bank.

"Maybe," Mark had told Saul, "if I can stay on the river with you long enough, the frogs will let me learn their language, too."

"Might be," Saul had said. "I started just like you; no bigger than a willow sapling."

Catlettsville was perhaps the only town on the Big Sandy River where the boys did not travel the riverbanks at night with flashlights searching for the great brown river frogs. Mark was largely responsible for this. Eager to learn the ways of the old man and the river, he had become the leader of the boys. They took catfish, perch, sucker, carp, and turtles from the river;

but they left the frogs for company, for the old man on the shantyboat.

It was the time of year when the white cotton blooms come to the river willows. Saul sat on the bow of the boat in a willow chair fixing nibs for the trotline he would soon set, when he heard a sound in the willows. Saul squinted his eyes and watched Sheriff Tarpin weave down the path. At the time, it did not seem strange for Sheriff Tarpin to come, so Saul waved his hand and quickly tied another nib to a fishhook. Boys had made the path, but men, too, traveled it to the shantyboat to learn the habits of the fish. Sheriff Tarpin was a fisherman, and he came often during the summer days to ask the advice of the old man. And then too, there were times that he came to ask about Mark, agreeing with Saul that the boy preferred the shantyboat to his home.

"Sometimes I wonder," Sheriff Tarpin had once told Saul, "if I'm raising a boy or a water dog. The other night I caught him in the backyard croaking like a bullfrog." Sheriff Tarpin had laughed out loud. "Doing a fine job of it too. I was on top of him before I could tell the difference."

Saul had chuckled at what Sheriff Tarpin had said. His chest had swelled with pride at the boy's doings. In the months since Mark had first come to the shantyboat, Saul had grown as close to him as the bark to the white flesh of the willow. Mark was smart and Saul had taught him to love the river. And there had been times when the boy's knowledge of the river had even

surprised the old man. Sheriff Tarpin had never object-
ed to the close relationship between the old man and
his son. He knew the vast store of knowledge the river
held. The river was a good life; a decent one.

Sheriff Tarpin crossed the board that Saul had put
from the bow of the boat to the bank. The old man
stared at the expression on the sheriff's face with his
squinted eyes and laid the nib aside. Sheriff Tarpin
scratched his head and fumbled with a piece of paper
he held in his hand. He took a seat in a willow chair
beside Saul. He fumbled with the paper some more,
and began to talk slowly. Judge Percy had asked him
to explain the contents of the paper to Saul, he began.
And his voice moved as slow as the lazy current of the
river.

The paper was a summons for Saul to appear in
Judge Percy's court. A warrant had been sworn by
Oliver Dodson, a wealthy man of the town, and a man
Saul hardly knew. In fact, a man to whom Saul had
never spoken, respectful as he was of the distance between a man wealthy enough to own much of the town
property and a man who owned only a driftwood
shantyboat. But the claim was, Sheriff Tarpin said,
that Dodson's only son, Cliptus Dodson, had been
threatened by death due to the influence of the old
man. A group of boys had dragged the Dodson boy
down the riverbank, dunked him in the blue river mud
and left him in the water to drown. According to Oliver Dodson's complaint the boys had been influenced
by the weird tales Saul told them; influenced to the

extent that they would threaten the life of another. The man who would set such tales in the minds of mere boys was incompetent and of an unsound mind.

"I've checked his story," Sheriff Tarpin said, looking out over the water. "Seems that the Dodson boy, on some sort of a dare, went to the river frogging, and the boys followed him down the bank. None of the boys will tell the reason for dunking him in the mud and leaving him in the water. I've questioned Mark and he's as mum as a tadpole. But, according to the Dodson boy, the trouble was over the tales of a frog. Something about your telling the boys a frog could talk. The Dodson boy said something about your being crazy and that he could prove it, and one thing led to another. Judge Percy said for you to be sure to know that Dodson is planning to prove that you're of an unsound mind. Feebleminded more-or-less I reckon is what I got to say. And that you ought to be sent somewhere where you can be watched over . . .

"Catfish biting yet?" he asked, then.

Saul pushed his long hair out of his eyes and looked upriver.

"Jest begin to leave the nest and come out of the creek," he said.

"Judge wants you there in the morning," Sheriff Tarpin said. "Knowing Dodson and all, I reckon he'll have his lawyer and things all ready. Coming out of the creek, are they? Don't forget the time. I sure hate to bring bad news. What bait do you reckon a man ought to use?"

"Soft crawdads," Saul said, staring at the slow-moving river.

Sheriff Tarpin walked the board and disappeared into the grove.

Saul laid a nib aside and picked up a willow branch that he had cut earlier to string his trotline around and started whittling on the end of it. A long, white shaving fell on the boards of the shantyboat and, pushed by the wind that drifted out of the willow grove, moved over the boards toward the end of the boat and into the river.

"River," Saul said, glancing into the shadows of the willows that drooped over the edge of the bank, "reckon that might be jest the way I'll soon be goin.' Jest that quiet and easy-like. Looks like them tales I told to the boys, meanin' no harm, has brung me trouble. Reckon, too, I learned the tales from you." He squinted his eyes and looked along the surface of the smooth water. "Guess I couldn't git mad and blame you, though. I've been with you all my life. Don't reckon I ever knowed nothin' else. Seems to me that I ain't got enough time left to be goin' somewheres else now. I'm in a heap of trouble."

Shadows covered the water and the moon came out and lowered its yellow beam and the river stretched out to sleep. From upriver drifted the croak of the great brown river frog. Saul sat down in the willow chair and crossed his hands over his knees. And he thought of leaving the river. To Saul it meant leaving a great friend on whom he had always been able to depend. The boys, of course, were his friends too, but Saul well knew that boys grew up and drifted away. There was less chance that the river would ever run dry. The boys had not come today and in so short a time Saul had begun to have a feeling of loneliness. Perhaps they would never come again. Maybe even Sheriff Tarpin would not allow Mark to come.

"Most times, River," Saul said, "I've told you my worries and you've showed me an answer. Reckon I'm askin' help again. It seems to be they's people what's thinkin' I ain't got the mind to care for myself no longer, and I reckon they're fixin' to git shed of me. And I reckon if it's these here river tales they're aimin' to ask about I jest ain't got an answer. I'm in a heap of trouble."

Saul leaned back against the cabin of the shantyboat and listened to the many sounds that came to the river at nights.

When he opened his eyes, the wind was high in the willows, and the sun had sifted through the clouds. He had slept far later that he had intended, but then most of the night he had twisted and had bad dreams. Once, in his dream, he had gone to Judge Percy's court and told everyone that he had been lying and teasing the boys about a frog being able to talk and he had been allowed to come back to the shantyboat. Then, in the next dream, one by one the boys had come down the willow path and stood in front of him with tears in their eyes. Mark had been the last to leave, staring at the old man with eyes he refused to believe that Saul had tricked him into believing a frog could talk. And

Saul had awakened knowing that he could never let the boys know he had lied. He could not forget the boys' faith and belief in him. It had been great enough for them to protect the great brown river frog so that the old man might have company at nights. Yet, actually Saul knew there was but one solution. He thought of it and closed his eyes and shook his head. He would tell the court about the tales and hope to convince them that he meant no harm. Maybe they would ignore the tales and let him return to the river. There was a chance that even Oliver Dodson might understand. The boys might not forgive him, and they might quit coming to the shantyboat, but at least he would have the river as his home. This much he knew . . . not to deny the tales would be a sure sight that he was of an unsound mind. He would not be talking to boys.

Saul splashed his face with river water and started up the path to town. He reached the dirt road and headed toward the city building, his head down. A man yelled and swerved his team of horses just in time to keep the wagon from hitting the old man. The man yelled again but Saul never raised his head.

Outside the courtroom door Saul stopped. He brushed his long hair out of his eyes, tucked his shirt into his pants, took a deep breath and walked in. The courtroom was crowded. Judge Percy squinted his eyes and looked toward the old man. Saul took another step and the squeak of his brogans, not worn since cold weather, drifted across the courtroom. With each step now Saul was reminded that he had forgotten to soak the brogans in river water to soften the leather and each squeak seemed to him as loud as the croak of a good-sized frog.

The back of the courtroom was filled with boys, most of them waving their hands as Saul looked back. Standing near the very back of the crowd was Mark, his eyes fixed on Saul as solemn as if he were studying the blue water of the Big Sandy. Saul recognized the faces of each of the boys. At the front of the room across from the chair in which the old man took a seat sat Oliver Dodson. Beside him was a tall, frail-looking boy wearing horn-rimmed glasses and looking as dignified as the man sitting on the other side of him with a briefcase across his lap. Saul figured this last man to be the lawyer Sheriff Tarpin had mentioned.

After Judge Percy had brought the court to order, the man with the briefcase stood up to address the judge and the court. He spoke words that Saul did not understand. It was only when he described Saul's weird tales that Saul understood. Even Saul himself had to admit the man had the stories down pat. He spent most of his time on the frog, stating that a man of sound mind could not possibly believe such nonsense. And then he informed the court that he would prove beyond a doubt by testimony of witnesses that Saul was not of sound mind. For the protection of the youth of the community he felt that the court should place such a man where he would be under the care of the proper authorities, where he could do no further harm.

As the man sat down, Judge Percy rubbed his chin, took off his glasses, cleaned them, and looked straight at Saul. Saul tugged at his pants, brushed his hair out of his eyes and stood up. He looked over the courtroom and rested his eyes on the boys in the back rows. Then he turned toward Judge Percy.

"Reckon," he said, "Judge Percy, I got somethin' to say. Reckon, too, I got to say it myself."

Several of the boys on the back row jumped up and clapped their hands. Judge Percy pounded on top of his desk and called his court back to order. Saul tugged again at his pants and looked toward the judge. Getting a nod from Judge Percy, he squinted his eyes and said:

"I ain't denyin' these here things that this man has said Mr. Dodson is accusin' me of. Guess most of 'em are as true as the water runs. I ain't educated enough to recognize all them big words that he used or know what they all meant, but I ain't goin' to say that he was right when he told you I ain't got mind to know what I'm doin'. Ain't no reason for him a-sayin' that, or sayin' I was meanin' harm by little tales I told about the frog. I don't reckon I ever brought trouble or harm to anyone."

"I object!" the lawer was on his feet.

"On what grounds does the counsel object?" Judge Percy said.

"Since it is our contention that the defendant is of unsound mind, his testimony would be of no value in the court's reaching a decision," the lawyer said.

Judge Percy scratched his head. He watched the old man tugging at the faded overalls for a minute, then looked out over the court.

"Objection overruled," he said, and nodded for Saul to continue.

"Ain't many here in this room," Saul said, "that don't know that I've lived all my life on the shanty-boat a-carin' for myself. Since I were big as a minnow I been fightin' that river to scuttle a livin'. River was kinda lonely like, 'cept when the boys come to visit me. Pa died when I was jest a boy, and I never had someone to set and tell me stories like boys like to hear. But I never asked help from anyone. I went right on workin' and carin' for myself. Most of the folks right here in your courtroom, Judge Percy, have bought willow chairs, bean and tomato stakes, catfish or turtle or somethin' other from me."

Saul scratched his head and pulled his pants farther up. "Don't reckon folks knowed of the times when I was the size of a willow sprout an' how it was to stand on the bow of the boat and watch other boys come to the river to fish and swim without a thing else to do. Don't reckon folks know either how I sit when the summer comes and watch the path for the boys to come to ask about the swimmin' holes and the fishin' holes and all sorts of things about the river. I know this river, and I can tell them most of the things they want to know. Why, Judge Percy, even you come sometimes to find where the catfish are."

Judge Percy cleared his throat, squinted his eyes across the courtroom, and looked down at the old man.

"Used to be that seein' someone smile at me was as

strange as seein' a spoonbill sturgeon here in the Sandy River. Not since the boys been comin' to the shantyboat, though, to listen to me and to ask me questions
'bout this river. Some of the answers . . . reckon I
sort of stretched . . . but I was meanin' no harm.
Guess it was jest that I didn't want 'em to know I
couldn't answer 'em when I knowed it made 'em happy
when I could.

"Now, 'bout this here frog Mr. Dodson is talkin'
'bout, reckon I can explain that. When the boys heard
the bellow of the river frog drift across the water, they
was wantin' to know what he were a-sayin'. I reckoned
I had to tell 'em somethin.' Frog will always answer
another croak this time of year, so I croaked back. If
I had thought for a minute that my stretchin' this here
frog talk was aimin' to cause trouble I wouldn't have
croaked. Guess this was where I done wrong. But if
it's this here frog a-talkin' that's causin' all the trouble,
I reckon maybe if I were to say that weren't none of it
true—" Saul looked toward the back of the room. One
of the smaller boys had fallen from the top of a bench.
No one helped him to his feet as the boys stared with
their mouths open. Saul tugged again at the overalls.
"Reckon that ain't what I'm aimin' to say, though.
Reckon I'm goin' to say that I told the boys a frog
could talk and if you was to know the frog language,
that you could talk back to him. Said that I could coax
a frog, I did, from the bank to the shantyboat and
into a burlap sack, and I reckon I could do it right
here in this courtroom as well, pervidin' I had a frog."

It was a full five minutes before anyone could be heard above the screams and yells of the boys in the back of the room.

"I object!" Mr. Dodson's lawyer was again on his feet.

"On what grounds?" Judge Percy said.

"What grounds, your Honor . . . on grounds that . . . this request is ridiculous," the lawyer said. "A frog in a courtroom as a witness? Would a man of sound mind make such a statement? Isn't this sufficient proof for the court?"

Judge Percy cleared his glasses again. He wrinkled his forehead and looked again at Saul. The old man stood, his chest out, a smile on his face, looking toward the boys.

"This court stands adjourned," Judge Percy said, clearing his throat, "until nine o'clock in the morning." He wiped his face. "At which time a frog will be brought into the court as evidence. I recollect nothing in any lawbook that prohibits a frog from entering a courtroom."

Under Judge Percy's direction a three-man committee was chosen to procure a frog. And Sheriff Tarpin was appointed to furnish the court with a common burlap sack.

Saul left the courtroom, his brogans squeaking, and walked the willow path back to the shantyboat. He sat in the willow chair, took off the brogans and wiggled his toes in relief. He thought how he had really piled a heap of trouble on himself now. Not only had he failed to tell the truth, which he had come to the conclusion was his only chance, but he had offered to prove in court that the tales he had told the boys were true. He knew that when he failed to do this, the court would be convinced that he was unable to care for himself on the river.

Why had he asked for all this trouble? He hadn't had to look toward Mark and the rest of the boys at the back of the courtroom. But he had. And it was when he looked into their faces that he knew he would never be able to let them know the tales were untrue. So he had made his decision. He had chosen to leave the river rather than let the boys know he had lied.

Saul sat lonely on the river and wondered where he would be sent. Maybe, he thought, it would be to a place where he would have to wear shoes all the time and wash every day. And then he would have to sit and dream of the Big Sandy River and the current of the water would be too far away for him to hear.

Saul closed his eyes, and he could see the great brown river frog sitting in the courtroom blinking its eyes from the lights overhead. The frog would be wondering the same thing as he: Would either of them ever get back to the river? Saul saw himself squatted on the floor, a sack in his hand. And when he croaked everyone in the courtroom would laugh and think he was crazy. There was little chance that the frog would even croak back, for it was seldom that a frog croaked during the daytime. There was one slim chance. With so many people in the courtroom the frog could get excited and jump. But the chance that it would jump into the sack was as thin as the fins of a catfish.

A strong breeze riffled the water and Saul heard the waves wash against the bank. Saul listened close as if he still thought that an answer would come. But nothing came, and at dusk the wind quieted. From the brush pile came the croak of the river frog. From below the boat out of a bed of snags came the answer of another. Saul looked at the river.

"River," Saul said, "maybe what I'm wantin' to know you jest ain't got the power to tell. But it seems to me they ought to be somethin' or other to help an old man what's in trouble because he wanted to make a bunch of boys happy. You've always give me an answer before. I reckon I'm askin' now harder than I ever asked before. Take your time because I reckon I intend to sit right here till daylight."

When morning came Saul rose from the willow chair and walked into his cabin. He splashed his face in a pan of river water and then made his way up the bank. On top of the bank he stood and looked out over the two rivers for a minute before he turned to walk to the city building.

Judge Percy called the court to order and ordered the frog to be placed about six feet from where Saul sat, a burlap sack at his feet. Saul eyed the frog. It was a green-colored frog. It blinked its eyes from the lights, looked around the courtroom, closed its eyes and squatted.

The small boys in the back of the room had climbed to the top of the benches and were trying to see over the heads of the older people up front. Mark stood at the end of the back row of benches moving around as

uneasy as a snag in river current. Saul glanced at the boys and unfolded the top of the sack. Then he quickly closed the sack, looked toward the judge and the courtroom and eyed the green frog for a considerable time. He looked up again at Judge Percy and then, turning his eyes again to the frog, he squatted on the floor. He opened the sack cautiously, never taking his eyes from the frog. He twisted his mouth to one side and a low sound drifted across the courtroom. The green frog opened its eyes, blinked, looked around the courtroom and then closed its eyes again. Saul curled his lip and another croak drifted over the room. The green frog remained motionless. Saul brushed his hair from his face. Oliver Dodson wiped the sweat from his neck. Judge Percy cleaned his glasses and everyone in the courtroom took a deep breath.

After a number of additional croaks, Mr. Dodson's lawyer was on his feet.

"I ask you, your Honor," he said, "hasn't the court had sufficient proof? This demonstration is ridiculous, and, if I might add, this courtroom is suffocating with heat."

Saul wrinkled his face and stood.

"I told the boys, Judge," he said, "that I could coax a frog into a sack, and I'm aimin' to do it. But this here ain't no ordinary frog. It ain't a river frog like the kind I am used to talkin' to. A river frog is brown and this frog is green. It's a creek frog. Judgin' the color, I'd say from up on Lost Johns Creek. That creek is strange water. And frogs is 'bout like us humans, I reckon. Folks on different lands talk different, and frogs on different waters talk different. They is a mite difference in the talk of a river frog and a creek frog. I got to have a little more time on this here frog." Saul scratched his head. "I ain't much in askin' favers, Judge Percy, but if I don't make this here frog jump into this here sack like I told it would, I reckon I ain't ever goin' back to my shantyboat."

Judge Percy studied the old man for a minute. He glanced at the people in the courtroom. Everyone had his eyes fixed on Saul. A boy fell from the top of a bench and the judge puckered his mouth.

"Take your time," Judge Percy said.

Saul opened the sack a little again and squatted to the floor. He curled his lip again and a croak drifted over the room. The green frog raised a little from the floor and looked toward the old man. And then slowly it rose. Everyone in the courtroom, including Judge Percy, rose slowly from their seats, their eyes on the frog. Saul curled his mouth again and a low, soft croak drifted over the room. The green frog pulled its front legs toward its stomach and leaped about six inches closer to Saul. The courtroom moved to the very edge of their seats. Judge Percy had his elbows on the far edge of his desk and even Mr. Dodson had moved closer. From the back of the room the small boy who had fallen off the bench fell again. This time he started to cry because another boy, bigger than he, crowded into his place on top of the bench.

Now, each time Saul curled his lip the green frog jumped closer. A foot and a half from the sack it stopped, squatted and closed its eyes. For the first time since the frog had began to leap Saul wiped sweat from his face.

It took a dozen more croaks before the frog opened its eyes again. Slowly it pulled its front legs toward its stomach. Saul opened the mouth of the sack and took a deep breath. He curled his mouth and leaned toward the floor. A soft croak lifted the frog. Its deep, coarse bellow almost shook the courtroom. Squatting as close to the floor as it could get, it leaped and landed inside the sack.

It was impossible to hear anything in the courtroom above the screams of the boys. They raced around the courtroom clapping their hands and shouting. Judge Percy banged on top of the desk and finally got them quieted down.

"It is the opinion of this court," he said, "that not only is Saul Stratton the most sane man in this courtroom, but that he is indeed a credit to this community as well as a gift to all the young people. This court stands adjourned." He cleared his throat and leaned toward the old man. "I want to see you, Saul, after the court has cleared."

When everybody had left the courtroom, Judge Percy walked around his desk and faced the old man. He stared at the sack in Saul's hand.

"Sure is a lot of jumping around in that sack," he said, bending over and looking into the mouth of the sack. He took a step backward and frowned. "Why," he said, "there's two frogs in there!"

A low bellow drifted out of the mouth of the sack,

follower by a deep, coarse croak. Judge Percy looked again. At the bottom of the sack sat a small brown frog. Beside it squatted the large green frog.

Saul squinted his eyes and looked toward the judge.

"Reckon they's somethin' I want to tell you, Judge Percy," he said. "It's 'bout this here other frog. I weren't intendin' to sneak away without your knowin' 'bout it. But you see, Judge, an old man like me ain't got no learnin' to git me out of trouble. Only thing I got is that river over there. Jest like you look to your lawbooks, I look to it for answers. I looked and looked last night and they was no answer in sight. I reckon I was mighty low when I walked into this courtroom. I don't reckon I rightly know where this other frog come from. All I know is that I opened the sack and there he sat, blinkin' eyes up at me. I knowed right off what to do, though. Pon-my-word, I says to myself, if that old river over there ain't gone and fetched me the an-swer I'm a-needin'. Maybe it's like you, Judge, when you hook one of them big mudcats. You ain't worryin' at the time 'bout where he come from. All you're thinkin' 'bout is how to git him in. I reckon it was wrong for me to squat here and act like I was croakin' when all the time I was pinchin' this here female frog makin' her croak and eggin' on that big male frog the committee brung. Frogs ain't much different from people, I reckon, when it comes to goin' a-courtin'. I knowed all the time I was doin' wrong, but I jest didn't have the heart to let all them boys know that I had been fibbin' to 'em. I figgered if I was goin' to be sent away that maybe you could do it sort of quiet and easy-like, not tellin' the boys, but jest lettin' 'em think that I jest took a notion and drifted downriver."

Judge Percy cleared his throat.

"Well," he said, "it is hard for me to believe that the river sneaked up here to the city building and put a female frog in that burlap sack. I am more inclined to believe that it was a human done the sneaking."

"Don't reckon I rightly know, Judge," Saul said. "That's the pure truth. But if a human did he would have to be someone that knowed a powerful lot about this river. He would have to know first off that it was the matin' season for the frogs. And he would have to judge that this here committee the court picked might not be carin' to get their feet wet when they went after the frog. He would have to be knowin' that it's the male frog that sits highest on the bank away from the water and that it would be him they'd be gittin'. And he would have to know that it would be a female frog he'd be needin' to sneak into the sack. That's a lot for a feller to know 'bout this river. I didn't even think of it myself right off."

"Still can't understand it," Judge Percy said, rubbing his chin. "Sheriff Tarpin got the sack and young Mark brought it over to the court just before the trial. Little fellow like him wouldn't know that much about the river, would he?"

"'Pon-my-word," Saul said, a smile crossing his wrinkled face. He chuckled out loud.

"What's that?" Judge Percy said, squinting his eyes at Saul.

"I—I say," Saul said, slowly, " 'pon-my-word, that would be a powerful lot for a little minnow like him to be knowin'."

"Well," Judge Percy said. "Either way I reckon you know that as judge of this court I will have to sentence you." He looked straight at the old man. "Withholding evidence is a criminal offense."

Saul stood up straight, holding the burlap sack in one hand.

"Sheriff Tarpin tells me," Judge Percy said, "that the catfish are coming out of the creek."

Saul nodded his head.

"I sentence you, Saul Stratton," Judge Percy said, "to one full can of soft crawdads to be used by me tomorrow on them catfish."

Saul let out the breath he had been holding during the sentencing and a smile crossed his face.

"Yes, sir, your Honor," he said. "I reckon I better be gittin' back to that river if I aim to be gittin' 'em before dark sets in." He turned away.

"One more thing, Saul," Judge Percy said. "Since young Mark is probably at the shantyboat, you better take him along and make that two cans of soft crawdads. Aiding a man when he is on trial without the knowledge or consent of the judge is equal to withholding evidence. That's just in case what I'm thinking might be right."

"Yes sir," Saul said.

The old man walked out the door and the squeak of his brogans drifted across the courtroom.

11.

Stubtoe the Champion

IT ain't like I don't know roosters. I've seen lots of gamecocks in my time. High-flying, hard-hitting, steel-gutted roosters shuffling from the head-waters of this valley to the mouth. But I ain't ever seen no rooster the equal of Stubtoe. That rooster could talk and he did. A seventeen-time winner he was and won most of them talking. Not talking like me and you talk, but chicken talk. Something I could understand, being close and all. Lots of men figgered me crazy the way I talked to that rooster when he was in the pit fighting, but them was the ones that took home a busted poke.

I remember the first time I ever laid eyes on old Stubtoe. You see, I had been up there at Cy Willard's barn picking game roosters killed in the pit. Every time one of 'em would get the steel put to him they'd sling him out of the pit with the death rattle in his throat and me and the other pickers would scramble for him. Cy would pay us a bull nickel for a picked rooster, and

you could make a little eating money. Cy always had
the dead roosters picked, supposedly for their owners
to take home and eat. But they never did take 'em,
and Cy knew they wouldn't. It seemed a favor, but
what Cy really did was have the roosters ground up at
the poultry house he owned in Sourwood, and he
passed them off in chicken salad to the uppitys of the
town who'd be eating leather-tough pit-fighting roosters like they was eating some little fluffity highfalutin
chicken. Well, I got paid for picking and not eating
and Cy said five cents to the man what grabs him first
and I'd scramble for that rooster with the best of them.

On this night I'd picked twenty roosters. The crowd
was heavy, the betting hard, and with the roosters that
was waiting to fight it looked liked we'd be going
through the day. We was still going strong when daylight
broke and I got up from the floor where I was sitting,
figuring that maybe I ought to get some fresh air and
work some of the stiffness out of my fingers. Maybe I
could pick faster when I came back, I thought. I
steps outside the barn door and I first sees old Stubtoe.
He was a nubbin of a chicken, about half grown, sad
and dirty-looking, not a heap of feathers to him. He
looked and sounded to me like he was about half dead
with the croup. His head was all hung down, and he
was hugging the barn like he was trying to dodge the
wind that was sweeping from the hills.

Well, I looked at that half-naked little rooster, and
he looked at me, and if I ever fell in love with a game
rooster, it was then. I mean I had found something in
my class, something that needed me as much as I

needed it, and I would've picked all the game roosters in Kentucky to've owned that sick chicken.

I mean ever since I'd picked my first rooster I'd wanted to own one. Maybe it was because of them long green bills I always seen passing between hands around the pit. Here I was picking chickens for five cents a head when if I owned my own rooster, I might win more money than I could count providing, of course, I didn't end up picking my own rooster. I was tired of just handling dead roosters. It was even dangerous, sometimes. One time in particular I remember: Cy flopped a big warhorse rooster out of the pit, and I scrambled and latched on to him. They had forgot to take the steel gaffs off him, and in the dying quivers he flopped and run a gaff clean through one of my hands. I got the scar right here to show it.

For whatever reason it might have been I went right back into the barn and asked Cy what he'd take for that rooster that was drooping around outside near the door. It was between pittings, and while they weighed more roosters up to be matched Cy goes to the door and takes a look. And mind you, it was then that my heart fell to my toes. That little rooster was a-laying flat of his back with his toes curled up, quivering like a fishing worm. He's done dead, I thought, and I got to my knees and picked him up. And if I live and breath that rooster looked at me and winked his eye.

Is he dead? Cy asks, looking at the little rooster in my arms. Nope, I say, but he's a-failing fast and one sick chicken, but I still want him. Well, Cy says, he

might be a sick chicken but he's a young fryer and who's to know a chicken is sick or not if I have him picked? Wouldn't have to grind that bird. He'd weigh out a sound dollar. But I'll tell you what I'll do: if you keep picking dead roosters till the fights end today, he's yours providing you get him away from my stock after the fights; he's liable to make the other chickens sick with his droppings. That little rooster wouldn't a-weighted out a dollar but I went back in and picked fifteen more roosters and I went home, packing my rooster of course.

For the rest of the summer all I done was pick roosters at night and talk to Stubtoe during the day. At first I had a hard time making out what he was trying to say, especially since he was growing up and his voice was changing. But by the end of the summer I could understand every word that rooster had to say. It was all chicken-talk, you understand, of course, and it come mostly with wanting to understand and closeness. He told me how he'd gone hungry back at Cy Willard's barn, and I could understand that since I'd gone hungry lots myself. And he told me how Cy's wife had throwed hot water on him one day at the back of their house. She was feeling ornery, and he was a cull, and she laughed at him because the water caused most of his feathers to fall out. There wouldn't be much picking to you, she said on seeing him after that. They thought he was just another rooster that had been hatched wild. I been laughed at before myself. But there was something they didn't know about Stubtoe.

All of the choice game roosters and hens was kept in wire pens. They was always fed real good while they raised their brood. The fighting chickens would come from these matches—Cy thought. The chickens that was left loose, to shift for theirselves, was said to be culls. Most of them was mixed breed and this would cause them to run when they got their first taste of steel in the pit. So none of the chickens outside the pens was ever used for fighting; they was used for egg laying and eating when company come.

But what they didn't know was that Stubtoe's daddy had been a champion. His mother had told him so. She had told him how she and his father had fell in love at first sight. All of the other barnyard hens had tried to tell her it wouldn't work out, but every day she would go to the wire pens and talk to him. One day he'd got out of the pens, and they'd gone into the hills to live. But it weren't for long; Cy had found Silverdip—that was him name—and had took him back to the wire pens. Through the long days on the nest, waiting for the eggs to hatch, Stubtoe's mother had grieved and wondered what had happened to Silverdip. Then one day one of the hens had passed and told her that Silverdip had been killed in the pit. Cy had fought him in the Battle Royal, which is where you put five roosters in the pit and the winner takes all. Silverdip had killed three roosters before he fell.

When Stubtoe's mother come back to the barnyard with her brood, the rest of the hens shunned her. They said she had gone above her raising. So, disgusted, she'd gone back to the hills to live and raise her family.

But she grieved herself to death before the family was grown. And finally all of the family had died off but Stubtoe. What ones hadn't been drowned in the hills during hard storms, the wild fox had caught. And if it hadn't been for me, Stubtoe said he would have died. Cy was a mean man. He didn't care about any of the chickens except the ones in the wire pens.

By the end of the cold winter Stubtoe was a grown rooster. His feathers was slick and shiny, and his long feathered tail was a sight to see in the early spring sun. He had all the color of his mother who had been part Warhorse and Allan Roundhead. But his white-tipped feathers were the markings of his father, Champion Silverdip, winner of seven fights in singles and three in the Battle Royal. Silverdip had been a large Dom.

One night, when I was getting ready to go up to Cy Willard's barn to do some picking, Stubtoe asked to go with me. I'm ready to fight, he says, just like my father fought. I want to avenge his death, and above all, I want to pay Cy Willard back for the way he treated my family. The only faver I ask is that you always match me against Cy's roosters. But Cy raises the best roosters in the hills, I said to Stubtoe. All champions. My father was a champion, that's what Stubtoe says to me.

I didn't want to take Stubtoe. I mean here I was living alone all these years in a little one-room shack in the head of Bocook Hollow, knowing the loneliness of the wind and the owls and the clouds and the rain. And then all of a sudden having something like Stubtoe to take all of that away. And I guess I couldn't understand him wanting to avenge his pa's death or having feeling for his old man. The only thing about my pa I could remember was that he was drunk and beat me a few times and that he drowned one day in the river and Ma died of consumption in the shack with only me to watch her and I was too little to carry her to the hole I had dug in the hill and a neighbor come at last to help me.

But I took Stubtoe with me that night, and he stood beside me while I picked chickens. And then about halfway in the night, just when I was picking a big black Warhorse that had got the steel put to him, Stubtoe looks at me and says: There he is in the pit. I looked over inside the pit and saw Cy standing up holding a big red rooster in his hands. Weigh up, he hollers. Who wants to match a chicken against the Red Devil? No one spoke up. Here's a chance to double that picking money of yours, Stubtoe says to me. Maybe triple it. How's that? I asks. Let me fight Red Devil, Stubtoe says. Let you fight Red Devil! I says. He's a nine-time winner. I doubt if Cy'll get a match for him here tonight. He's some rooster, I says. Look at them feathers shine! Well, Stubtoe says, there is more to a rooster than feathers.

I don't rightly know what ever made me to it, but I hollers and tells Cy that I would match him. I walks over into the pit. That is I'd match you, I says, if I had a set of steel gaffs for my rooster. Cy just laughs. Well, he says, I see you got that rooster feathered out some. And I see that you want to pick him too. Well,

I guess if nobody here wants to match a rooster against me I might as well let my bird warm up on that cull you got. He ain't a sickly bird, is he?

Cy hands me a set of steel gaffs and he looks over the crowd and laughs. How much will you get for picking your own chicken? someone yells. Yep, they called me a chicken picker which I was and Stubtoe a cull which he weren't. I've got four dollars, Cy, I says . . . and to make it more interesting, he says to the crowd, I'll pick my own rooster if he loses. Pick him right here where the crowd can watch. Why you never heard such a laugh as went up around the pit.

If you lose, Stubtoe, I says, I won't do you like the other owners do their roosters and wring their heads off. Not even if you run. Stubtoe just says: My father didn't run. And I set Stubtoe down on the sawdust floor of the pits, and he struts before the crowd, looks at me and winks and then walks to the center of the pit. I put my hands over my eyes and the crowd hollers. Stubtoe is dead, I think. Nothing but a bird to some people but the only thing I ever really had or owned in my life that was something.

But when I looks up Cy is holding Red Devil in his hands near the edge of the pit and blood is dripping from the rooster's bill. Stubtoe pokes his head high into the air and crows. He strutts over to me. Collect your money, he says.

Cy was trying best he could to put life back in his rooster for another round. He puts his mouth over the Red Devil's bill and sucks the blood out and spits it on the sawdust. You see the Red Devil was rattled. Stubtoe had set his gaffs into the rooster deep causing Red Devil to bleed from the inside, and Cy's only hope was to suck the blook out quickly so's his rooster could breathe. And while he's doing this the crowd is booing Cy. Put the rooster down, they yells. Let him fight if he's got life in him. Cy works hard. He licks the big rooster's feathers back into place and hopes for life, but the rooster's gone. And when I leave the barn the crowd is hollering for Cy to start picking.

Well, don't you know that during the next two summers old Stubtoe went on to win seventeen fights. He'd always talk to the rooster he was fighting—he told me—getting them mad and careless and then putting the steel to them. Chickens is like folks in this way, I told Stubtoe: get a feller mad, and he'll lose his head and give you the advantage. I was offered lots of money for that rooster time and time again. I just laughed off the offers. Stubtoe wasn't like a chicken to me at all. I mean we was something, the two of us. And we had never been something before. Everyone said they was some sort of magic betwixt me and that rooster. But it weren't nothing but chicken and human talk mixed up—the kind you get by just being together and looking each other in the eye, a knowingness in sight and touch and smell.

Everything was going all right until one night— one cold winter night—I heard Stubtoe scratching around outside the window to the room where I slept. He always roosted in the big oak in the yard since he said living out in the weather kept him in condition. I went out to take a look and found Stubtoe on his side

in the deep snow. His feet was frostbit. I carried him
into the house and did everything I knowed to save
him. And I did. I mean I saved his life, but the cold
bit off the ends of every one of his toes. That's how he
come to have the name Stubtoe. I'd always just called
him Rooster in the beginning, but it was Stubtoe that
stuck in the end.

All the rest of the winter Stubtoe just dropped
around. When spring come I went back to picking
chickens more regular. I never took Stubtoe with me.
But every morning when I come home I'd set down
and tell Stubtoe about every one of the fights that had
been fought that night. And I could see that he was
a-grieving something awful.

Then one morning when I come home Stubtoe was
out strutting like a young stag rooster. He said that he
knowed that tonight was the night they would fight
the Battle Royal up at the barn, and I said that I
believed that it was, knowing that it was but hoping
he was beginning to forget about fighting again. Let
me fight in it, he says. This is the one fight I been
waiting for. This was the fight my father was killed in.
I said, But you know as well as me, Stubtoe, that the
Battle Royal is the toughest of them all. Well, Stubtoe
says I been telling him that for three summers now
and he things I figger now with his toes off he ain't
got a chance. And I says that some of what he says is
true, especially about the toes. But he says that he's
had the long winter to think and plan for this fight.
And he knows that for a game cock what's been cut

by steel he's an old bird and this will be his last chance. Let me fight this one last fight, he says.

I spent the day trying to talk him out of it, but when I left for the pit that night I took him with me. He was acting spry and sassy. For me, I figgered. But he did seem calm and blinking at me not to worry.

It all made me so nervous at the pit that I could hardly pick the dead roosters and got outscrambled for the better part of them. It hurt me to see the people staring at Stubtoe's feet, some grinning. But old Stubtoe just stood there beside me paying no attention and waiting for the Battle Royal.

When the time came, I was almost too nervous to take him inside the pit. The crowd was grinning more now and trying for bets. Cy steps inside the pit holding the pride of the wire pens—Big Blackpay, a fifteen-time winner even if poorly tested. Cy had never tried to match Blackpay with Stubtoe before, but Stubtoe had had all his toes then. Cy says to me, I see the feathers are coming off that rooster again, this time with age ain't it? Looking at his feet I'd say they ain't much chance he can run. The crowd was all fired up, and they liked that. So Cy, knowing he had the crowd, said, One more thing before the fight—if Stubtoe loses will you pick your bird before the crowd like I done once? I thought, how could I do a thing like that, pick Stubtoe. It would be like taking a knife and skinning myself. But then, I thought, Stubtoe is a champion. He'd been a champion all the way, and if he was willing to fight four roosters with nothing but stubs to hold him up, I wasn't about to let him think that I figgered him to lose. So, I tells Cy in front of all the people that I would pick my rooster if he lost.

I set Stubtoe down inside the pit. He looked at me and winked like he'd always done before each fight. But it weren't the young wink that he had had before. A lot of the shine had left his feathers and he was the oldest rooster in the pit.

Into the middle of the circle the roosters went. That is, all of them but Stubtoe. He just went walking off slow as a turtle, keeping to the rim of the pit, his head high and proud. Watching all the moves the other roosters made. One rooster in particular: Cy's champion, Blackpay. Blackpay had gone off as a ten-to-one favorite; Stubtoe fifty to one. And now the crowd was laughing as old Stubtoe hugged the rim of the pit. They shouted: Better get him out of there before he gets scared to death. He's had too much steel put to him. We knowed he was part cull all the time. All sorts of things.

But it didn't bother Stubtoe. He just waited, his proud old head still high in the air. He stood there so long that even I began to worry. Is he really scared! I wondered. He sure ain't making no shine to fight. And when there's but two roosters left out in the pit he's still standing there at the rim, not offering to fight. And then the two roosters went high in the air, shuffled and one fell dead and one landed alive and that live one was Blackpay. Big Blackpay strutted like a rooster will do to a hen, circling the last of the dead roosters. And then he turned to crow, facing the side of the pit opposite from Stubtoe. I don't reckon he even knowed Stubtoe were in the pit, or maybe he wasn't thinking him worthy of a look. I looked down at Stubtoe and Stubtoe winked. He moved toward the center of the pit, behind the big rooster. Cy hollered, but it meant nothing to Blackpay. You got to be close to a rooster for him to understand human talk and to Cy a rooster was only business. The crowd yelled. And big Blackpay did turn. But it was too late. Stubtoe had sunk his gaffs deep into the rooster's breast and the blood dripped from Blackpay's feathers. His crowing ended in a death rattle. Stubtoe hopped up on the rooster and crowed, and his crow was high and piercing and old. But under the lights hanging from the beams in the barn his feathers had a shine to them. And he looked every bit like the old champion that he was. I got all choked up and couldn't hardly see to carry him from the pit. Everyone was yelling that he was the greatest champion of them all, the best that ever lived, and the old rooster was touched by it, too.

Stubtoe didn't live long after that. Died a champion, he did. I told him I'd follow soon after him not to worry none but be looking. I mean they ain't no reason why chickens and people ain't going to the same place that I can figger.

12.

The Fiddle and the Fruit jar

PA'S fiddle hung in its case from a rusted nail on the wall of the bedroom. This had been its resting place since the day he and Ma had first gone to housekeeping in the valley of the Big Sandy. And through the years it had remained the only competition that my mother ever had. I say competition because it was often declared here by the hill folk that a fiddle player had a wanderer's foot. You could not change the ways of a fiddle player. Ma knew this. And so as a young bride she allowed the fiddle to become a part of their marriage. In all of Pa's travels over the valley the sweet music of his fiddle would be loved the most at home. Ma presented him with eight children, more than a good set for a square dance, and in all the years of our growing up I'm sure that the fiddle never caused her a jealous moment.

After Pa came home from work at his small cobbler's shop we used to gather in the center of the floor and wait for the music of his lonesome fiddle. We

learned early that there was a story in each of his ballads. We couldn't afford books, but we learned to read
each pull of his bow as if it were a printed page.

Each night ended the same way, with the eight of us
quarreling for Pa to play a different ballad. And always Ma would scold and threaten to have Pa put the
fiddle back in the battered case. Afraid he might, we
quieted as Pa pat-patted his foot and struck up an old
familiar song . . . Ma's favorite. He was sure to play
this song as soon as a frown touched Ma's face, grinning and bringing a smile back to her face.

The song was a ballad of love, so bold that it made
my older brothers and sisters blush. I was too young
to understand love. I liked to hear Pa play it simply
because it brought such smiles to Ma's face, and gave
me courage to argue again for my favorite song.

By the time I was old enough to really know my
father he had fiddled his hair white to match the white
pine rosin dust that his bow had left under the strings.
The fiddle had traveled with him over every foot of the
Big Sandy country; to square dances where feet flew
into the air like brown leaves in an autumn wind; to
funerals where his fiddle hummed of death; to holy
baptizings in the waters of the Big Sandy River. There
had been ballads for all occasions. Pa had gained the
reputation of being the greatest of the "old-time fid-
dlers" among the hills of Kentucky.

But now white-haired Pa was farther away from
his fiddle than he had ever been. Only his dreams could
touch it as it hung inside the battered case on the
wall. He was bedfast from a stroke, the third within

a year. He lay quarreling over the doctor bills coming, saying Ma needed the meager amount of money to buy food for the table.

The doctor had not given much promise. Either of the first two strokes had been great enough to have killed Pa. But he had proved by two recoveries that he was as stubborn and tough as the hills around him. This was the best encouragement the doctor could give.

But Ma had caught something in Pa's eyes that the doctor could not see. It was not the paralyzing of his body she saw there, but the paralyzing of his mind and spirit.

In the days that followed, Ma rested her eyes often on the battered fiddle case. She attributed untold powers to it, believing that if she could coax Pa to find courage to take it from the wall the pull of the bow over the strings would strengthen and mend his body. But Ma had less time now for coaxing. She left the house early to find housework. She scrubbed floors on her hands and knees, and stretched her little body to wash down walls. Of the evenings she brought home baskets of clothes and washed them with her hands into the late night. These hours of labor brought us food. And she sat on the edge of Pa's bed and fed him as she would have a small child, knowing that each bite he took reminded him of his helplessness and paralyzed him a little more.

It was not easy for Pa to remain flat on his back. He had worked hard all his life. He had begun in the small belly mines of the mountain country, then found his craft as a shoe cobbler. He had learned to work miracles with his hands. Weaving the needle in and out of leather that he had softened by hand, he built shoes for clubfooted children and covered scars and afflictions that couldn't be shod by machine-made shoes.

It shamed me to see an old man such as Pa have tears in his eyes as Ma fed him. Never once did it occur to me that he might have been looking at my mother's red hands, cracked until they bled over the rough washboard. Or that he might have been thinking it was a man's place to bring food to the table. I knew only that he had told me over the years that I should feel ashamed for crying. A *man* never cried.

One evening Ma came home from work and found the fiddle gone. She trembled as she spoke to Pa. "Where is the fiddle?"

Pa fought to raise his hand and Ma reached to take it in hers. And when they met Pa slipped something to her. She unfolded the wrinkled dollar bills and they fell to the floor.

"You . . . you had no right to do it," she sobbed. "I'm no better to provide than you've been doing all these years." And she could not say more.

Pa never was much of a talker. "A talking man never hears," he had always taught us kids. And without practice himself he failed miserably on this night. He could not convince Ma that he would remain paralyzed forever. She cried softly, believing that the only medicine to cure him was now gathering dust in the corner of the secondhand store—sold for little more than she could have earned with a few washings. Yet this pitiful sum had made Pa believe he had lightened Ma's burden. His eyes, wandering to rest on the rusted nail, sadly told us that what he had done had not been easy.

Often of the evenings I would go to meet Ma and help her carry the washings home. I was the smallest of four boys and the only one too young to be ashamed of being seen carrying them, telling all within sight that we were as poor as the red clay hills around us.

Each day Ma stopped at the secondhand store, leaving me outside guarding the clothes. This was one of Ma's queer new ways I could not understand. For instance, a few days earlier I had seen her stuffing something inside an empty fruit jar in the basement and then hiding the jar. After she had gone I sneaked the jar into the open and saw money in it. I just could not understand why she would be hiding money from us when there was so little to eat.

I sneaked each evening to see the jar until she finally caught me. She said, "What little money there is inside the jar wouldn't fill your tooth. It's the love tucked around it that fills the jar."

It just didn't make sense. I didn't know that old people had love. I thought it belonged only to the young, like my brother who was sparking a girl who lived nearby.

I went with Ma the morning she took the money from the jar. After we had picked up a heaping basket of clothes to be washed we stopped at the secondhand store. I stood guarding the basket and she went inside.

When she came out she had the battered fiddle case under her arm. She tucked it under the clothes, and warned me not to speak of it when we reached home.

That night Pa quarreled at Ma for spending her hard-earned money to bring the fiddle back to just gather dust on the wall. But his tired old eyes had changed and they lied on him this time. There was tenderness inside them that we all recognized as we peeked around the door.

Ma scolded us back to bed and we cocked our ears hoping to hear the fiddle again. But no sound of music came. Since I was the smallest and the lightest on foot I was chosen to sneak again to the door and tell what I saw.

Here is what I told them: I saw my father lift his arm by his own strength and brush tears from my mother's eyes.

He tried to play the fiddle. He tried to play Ma's favorite . . . the one he always used to put her in a happy mood . . . the song he had first played many years ago when he had come to court her. And although we heard nothing but the squeak of the bow held by a crippled hand, I think that to them it was the softest, sweetest ballad he had ever played.

In the years that followed, Pa teased Ma about pulling him from the grave just to listen to his fiddle. Ma always blushed. She had little time for *foolishness*. She was always too busy spreading her love among us . . . the same sort of love she had tucked around the money inside the fruit jar.

13.

Lucy Caught the Moon

JEB stood by the window and looked down the narrow path that wound like a brown snake through the willow saplings on the banks of Cattlett's Creek. It would be along this path, he knew, Uncle Jeptha would come, his big shoulders pushing the willow limbs out of the path. In front of him, swishing her long tail, would be his little redbone hound, Lucy. Lucy would not be bringing a pup with her this time, according to Jeptha; that would come later. Today, Jeptha was coming to tell Jeb how he was to earn the pup Lucy was going to find.

Every time the wind lifted the willow limbs along the path Jeb caught his breath and waited. He held his breath until the wind died and the willow limbs swayed back in place. Ever since Jeptha had told Jeb, on his last visit, about earning the pup, Jeb had done little but think about it. Maybe, he thought, Jeptha would ask for money, and there were not many ways a boy could earn money here in the mountains this time of year.

From the signs of the sky, Grandma Quildy said the water from the creek would rise over the banks early and flood the bottoms. Ground would be broken late and there would be little work in the fields until midsummer. By that time, Jeb would be too busy raising the garden at the house to work for neighbors. Jeptha would be upriver cutting the tall trees and rafting them to float down the mouth of the Big Sandy River and he would not be home to help with the garden. Grandma Quildy was old and her bones were brittle and her skin was wrinkled and she could not do much work.

Jeb turned from the window and looked toward the fire grate. Grandma Quildy sat in her rocking chair reading her Bible. The flame from the fire shadowed her face and her long, gray hair. But Jeb was thinking now of the pup.

"Grandma Quildy," Jeb said, "do you reckon Uncle Jeptha will come today?"

"Before dark if the Lord's willing," she answered, placing a pine split between the pages and closing the Book. She looked toward the window and squinted her eyes at the dark clouds hovering over the steep ridge above the house.

The coulds came every year at this time, and Jeptha came from the hills every year at the same time. And always Jeb stood by the window and waited. Grandma Quildy would mumble a prayer that Jeptha be guided along the tramroads to the cabin.

Jeptha was a big man and Jeb knew that he knew the hills. He had helped build most of the tramroads. When the creek would rise early, Jeptha knew the shallow places to cross. A man as smart as Jeptha would need little help from the Book.

There were many things Jeb didn't understand about the Bible. When he was small, Grandma Quildy had told him that this Book had guided his mother and father up the steep hill path to the ridge to rest for a while, and the Book had sent him to live with her. This Book had placed a cover of earth over his father and mother to shield them from the snows of the winter and the sun and rain of the summer. And one day the Book would lead them all to a home beyond the clouds.

One day Jeb asked her if hound dogs lived beyond the clouds and she told him she couldn't find any print in the Book that said so. And he told her if there wasn't he didn't believe he would care to go there and she scolded him. He asked Jeptha about it and was told that Grandma Quildy's eyes were failing with old age and she couldn't see the print in the Book too well to find the answer to questions like Jeb's.

"How would you be able to hunt if there were no hound dogs there?" Jeptha had asked.

It was dusk when Jeptha came up the path. The black clouds had opened and emptied the rain, and when he came through the door, he was soaking wet. He walked to the fire and Grandma Quildy handed him a towel. She told him she had been worried about his coming home during the time of a storm.

"Swam the creek with one hand and guided Lucy with the other," Jeptha said, laughing and rubbing the towel through his hair.

The door cracked and Lucy stood with her nose just inside. She held her head low and turned her eyes toward Jeptha. Her tail made a thumping noise against the side of the door.

"Come in, Lucy," Jeptha said, looking toward Grandma Quildy, knowing Lucy would track water over the floor and shake more from her hair.

Lucy came farther into the room. Her hair was parted by the rain from her nose to her tail. She was the prettiest hound Jeb had ever seen, even though Grandma Quildy had said her tail seemed too long for just one dog. Her hair was the color of the redbird, and her eyes as black as the sparrows. Her tail *was* long, the longest that Jeb had seen on just one dog.

Once, Jeptha had told Jeb he could have sold part of Lucy's tail. A man at the timber mill named Chet Potter had asked to buy it. Chet's sister had sent him a bulldog from over in West Virginia and it had come to the hills without a sign of a tail on it. Hardly even a short stub. "Now whoever heard of a dog without a tail here in the mountains?" Jeptha had said. Chet had been kidded so much about the tailless dog that he had offered to buy part of Lucy's, according to Jeptha. He had intended to sew part of it onto the stub of the bulldog, just like grafting a limb to a tree. "Now whoever heard of a red-tailed bulldog here in the mountains?" Jeptha had asked.

It didn't seem possible. Still, Jeb had seen Japtha graft limbs to trees and make them grow and so he was not sure. But if it were true, he was glad that

Jeptha had not sold Lucy's tail. A bobtailed hound would look funny, and then, too, a hound could well be judged by the swish of its tail.

Jeb sat at the table waiting for Jeptha to eat. He was not hungry himself, yet he knew he must wait until Jeptha had finished before he could ask about the pup. Hound dog talk had no place at an eating table according to Grandma Quildy. But when Jeptha filled his plate again, Jeb became restless and said, "I want to ask you something, Uncle Jeptha."

"Not at the table," Jeb," Grandma Quildy said.

Jeptha finished the plate and pushed it into the center of the table.

"Reckon we'll have to go into the other room to talk," he said.

Jeb followed Jeptha in by the fire grate and looked back toward the other room for Grandma Quildy.

"I reckon," Jeptha said, "what you want to ask concerns this pup that Lucy is about to find."

"Reckon," Jeb said, scooting closer to the chair where Jeptha sat.

"Been doing some thinking about the pup," Jeptha said. "Ought to be a powerful pup, you know." Jeptha wrinkled his face and rubbed his chin. "Good hound pup is worth a heap of money here in the mountains. Man from the mountains has about got to have a hound dog. They all can't have one like Lucy and the pup will probably be about as close to her as you can get. That's the way I got it figured. Some of the men at the timber mill have asked me to set a price. Chet Potter has put a high bid already."

"Maybe he's only after the tail," Jeb said, still wondering if it were possible.

"Maybe," Jeptha said. "It's not my concern to ask what he wants the pup for; it's his money and once sold the pup is his."

Jeb looked at Lucy. She was curled close to the fire.

"Grandma Quildy says the creek will rise early this year," Jeb said. "I won't be able to find work in the bottoms until up in summer. But I'd be willing to work earlier. I could go back to the mill with you and stay until I made enough to earn the pup."

"Couldn't do that," Jeptha said. "Got to be someone here to look after things."

Jeb looked toward the kitchen where Grandma Quildy was washing dishes. He was thinking that if he had to stay home and work, then by rights Grandma Quildy should help him talk for the pup. But then, he thought, she had not been concerned about his getting the pup. Whenever he tried to talk with her about it, she would always just say that hound dog talk belonged between men. It was men-talk only.

Jeb looked toward the fire, toward where Lucy lay. He knew he could not bid with Chet in money.

"There might be a way, though," Jeptha said. "Money is good to have but it's not the only thing. Good, hard work goes a long way with me. By the time I come again, the creek will be swollen over the bottoms. Carp will be swimming upcreek from the river and you know how I like to take a spell at catching a mess. Bait could be the only thing to slow me down."

"I could get the bait," Jeb said. "Lots of it." And

with the thought that this could be a way of earning
the pup, Jeb spoke quickly. "I could get red worms. I
know where they bed." And Jeb was thinking of the
rich earth beside the barn, kept soft and warm by the
bedding hay he put there during the winter.

"Not worms," Jeptha said. "Worms aren't carp bait.
When winter covers the bottoms, worms are brought
to the top, out of the ground, and the carp will get all
they want. They get independent when it comes to
worms. But! Say a man was to have some doodlebugs.
Now that would be real carp bait."

Jeb thought of the doodlebugs. They were small,
white worms similar to the grubworm in many ways.
Their home was underground, generally away from the
low bottoms, and there was only one way they could
be caught. With a straw. Like the crawdads, they dug
into the ground and left an opening on top. Once you
found a hole, you poked a straw into it and twisted the
straw around easy. If the doodlebug was there, he
would move the straw and try to push it out of the hole.
If you pulled easy on the straw, you could draw him
to the top and grab him. If you pushed too hard, or
twisted too hard, you would push the straw through
the tender skin of the doodlebug and kill him. But
first of all the ground had to be warmed by the sun
before the doodlebug would stir, and it was still early
in the year. The sun was still slow breaking through
the leafless oaks on top the ridge.

"How many doodlebugs?" Jeb asked, thinking of
the few he had been able to catch the year before.

"Maybe twelve," Jeptha said. "That's not many for Lucy's pup. But we can throw your work around here in for good measure."

"That's a heap of doodlebugs," Jeb said, "with the ground still thawing."

"The pup will be a heap of hound, too," Jeptha said. "Of course, it could be more work than you want to do. Bids are still coming in at the mill. But I figure Chet Potter to stay high. Maybe the tail, and maybe not."

Jeb thought of the twelve doodlebugs he would have to catch. And then he thought of the hound pup walking around at the timber mill to be laughed at because its tail was gone. He was not sure of this growing a tail on a bulldog, but whether it grew or not, the tail would still be cut off the pup leaving it a bobtailed hound. He had never questioned Jeptha's knowledge when it came to hounds. He figured Jeptha knew about all there was to know about them. Lucy was proof of that.

"I can catch the doodlebugs," Jeb said.

"Think about it tonight," Jeptha said. "If at daylight, when I leave, you still don't believe it's too much work to catch them, you can have your chance to earn the pup."

And at daylight Jeb was more determined than ever to catch the doodlebugs. Grandma Quildy looked toward the spotted sycamore that stood at the edge of the yard. Jeb knew she was judging the wind by the sway of the naked limbs. By judging the wind, she could know how soon the heavy rains would return. Jeptha looked toward the same sycamore and then toward Grandma Quildy.

"I should be at the mill ahead of the rain," he said.

Jeb walked as far as the willow grove with Jeptha, talking about the pup all the way.

"I'm depending on you, Jeb," Jeptha said, "to watch after your Grandma Quildy. She's getting old and you'll have to do most of the work. These doodlebugs will have to be on your own time."

Jeb stood until Jeptha and Lucy were out of sight, and then he turned back toward the cabin. Grandma Quildy sat in the rocking chair reading the Bible.

"A dozen doodlebugs aren't too many, are they, Grandma Quildy?" Jeb said.

"Poor doodlebugs," Grandma Quildy said. "Taken from the ground to be skinned on a hook."

Jeb didn't think that Grandma Quildy wanted to talk about the doodlebugs, so he walked to the creek to gather driftwood. He sat a long while under the willows listening to the creek water.

The sun was disappearing from the slope and birds had begun to chatter. Jeb wondered if the birds chattered because the sound of the water over the rocks kept them awake. They flew from limb to limb, as restless as the wind. Once he had thought if he listened long enough, he would be able to know what the birds were saying. But now that he had grown older, he knew he would never really know. Nor would he ever understand the talk of the water. Not even Jeptha knew these things, and Jeptha knew most of the signs and sounds of the mountains. There were many things about the dark mountains that no man could ever learn.

The sound of the water running over the rocks, Jeb thought, was the prettiest of all the sounds of the hills. It was company to Jeb. Sometimes it was very lonely at the cabin.

The next day it began to rain heavy, and a week passed before the rainy weather broke. The black clouds disappeared and the sun began to sift early through the oaks on the ridge. But it had been a cold winter and the ground was frozen deep. It would take a lot of sun to draw the coldness from the earth. The black loam along the creek would be the first to warm; it would take the sun longer to break through the clay on the mountain.

But Jeb knew he would not be able to doodle for the doodlebugs in the black loam because of the rising water. The thawing of the frozen ground and the heavy rains had already begun to push the creek over the bottoms. His doodlebugs would have to come from the hillsides. The garden patch would be his only chance. Made soft by last year's plowing, it would not be as hard as the clay.

Jeb began to work the hillside above the cabin, clearing the ground. And while he grubbed the ground of saw briers and honeysuckle, he looked for doodle-bug holes. When he found a hole, he would lay the hoe aside and squat to the ground with a straw. He twisted and moved the straw slowly. But the only movement was from the wind moving down the ridge, weaving the straw back and forth. The holes he found were smooth and level on top and he knew that these were old holes and that the doodlebugs had left with the coming of last winter's snows. A soft hole would have a fresh mound of dirt around it where the doodlebug had shoved it out digging the hole. But there would be little time and he knew that he must try every hole if he were to catch twelve.

A week passed before Jeb spotted the first fresh hole. It had been dug close to the roots of a black oak standing at the edge of the garden patch. Jeb stretched on his stomach and eased a straw into the hole. He twisted slow and waited. The wind quivered the straw and Jeb jumped. For a minute then, he was mad. He took a deep breath. He knew he was too anxious and had been fooled by the wind.

This time he cupped one hand in back of the straw to shield off the wind, twisted the straw and waited. The straw moved, and Jeb eased it toward the top of the ground. He could feel the weight of the doodlebug and his heart beat fast. He spotted the head of the doodlebug above the hole and moved his hand fast to cup it just as the doodlebug let loose of the straw and slid back into the hole. Jeb had grabbed too fast, not letting the doodlebug come out far enough. Now the doodlebug would be wise and harder to fool. But Jeb knew that he had to have him. He eased the straw into the hole again, twisted and waited. But the straw did not move. He twisted again and waited. Again there was no movement.

Maybe, Jeb thought, the end of the straw has split

and could not reach the end of the hole. It was for sure that the doodlebug was all the way to the bottom. He pulled the straw out and looked at the end. The end of the straw was feathered and it was wet. Jeb felt the straw and wrinkled his forehead. He knew he had been too anxious. The straw had been pushed through the tender skin of the doodlebug and now it could never be brought out. He thought of the doodlebug lying dead at the bottom of the hole, picked up the hoe and moved it slowly over the tough pods of grass. It seemed he would never catch any doodlebugs.

The next day Jeb's hopes went higher; he spotted and brought the doodlebug out. He fumbled it with his hand and looked at it for a long time. It was like holding a piece of money and, Jeb thought, had been harder to earn.

That evening he took the doodlebug home, put it in a box of black dirt and sneaked it into his room, hiding it under the eaves of the roof. When darkness came he lay awake and listened to the sparrows chatter outside the eaves. He could not sleep, thinking that there was a chance the sparrows knew the doodlebug was in the box and when he was asleep they would find a way into the eaves and get it.

Jeb spotted the next doodlebug hole under a pod of grass. He had started to grub away the grass when he spotted the fresh mound of dirt. He lifted the blades and eased the straw. And up came the doodlebug. Before the sun set below the oaks, Jeb had caught four. That made five all together. Seven more to go.

In three days he would have to turn the ground to

plant seed, and there would be no doodlebug holes left
to spot—only the long, red clay furrows. Outside of
the garden patch the ground would still be hard, not
loosened by the plow, and some coldness would still
be under the hard crust. There were not likely to be
new holes. But he could not shun his work because
Jeptha had said the doodling must come on his own
time. Grandma Quildy was depending on the garden
and seed had to be planted.

Jeb sneaked the four doodlebugs to the box in his
room, and went to bed early. Tomorrow he would have
to have keen eyes and watch closer than ever for fresh
holes.

And at daylight he stood along the slope of the
hill and watched the sun sift through the budded limbs
of the oaks. He bent over the hoe, scanning the ground
close, until his back ached. When he came to a large
pod of grass or honeysuckle he stopped and lifted the
leaves aside searching for a hole. By the end of the day
he had found only one. And from this hole he coaxed a
doodlebug almost too small to cover a hook. He put
the doodlebug in his hand, covered it with dirt and
walked toward the cabin. Before he was off the slope
he could see Grandma Quildy standing in the yard,
looking toward him.

"Jeb," she said, "I'm ashamed of you, putting
doodlebugs in your room. The house is no place for
worms. Something just told me to look close to the
eaves."

"But Grandma Quildy," Jeb said, "the doodlebugs

are in a box and they can't climb out. Doodlebugs can't climb like red fishing worms."

"The house is still no place for them," she said. "And you'll have to take them out. I'm not going to touch a box of worms."

"Where can I put them?" Jeb asked. "I got to watch them. Jeptha will be here any day now, and I can't catch many more."

"You don't have to watch a box of doodlebugs," Grandma Quildy said. "I never heard of a person stealing doodlebugs. Either out they go or the chickens get them. I won't sleep another night in there with the thought of worms crowling around."

Jeb took the box of doodlebugs from his room and walked into the yard looking for a safe place to hide them. If he put them far from the house he wouldn't be able to watch them. And if he kept them too close Grandma Quildy would be apt to feed them to the chickens. He looked toward the woodpile under the big sycamore. He could see the woodpile from the window of his room, and it looked like the only place. During the day he could take the doodlebugs to the slope with him and during the night when the moon was bright he could watch them from the window. On dark nights he would have to take his chances.

Jeb made a flat place on the woodpile and placed the box there. He laid a flat board over the box to shield the doodlebugs from rain that might come without warning. And while he placed the box Jeb saw Grandma Quildy's dominecker rooster scratching in the dirt below the woodpile, turning his head sideways and watching him. Jeb threw a stick at it, and it ran around the house.

"You get my doodlebugs," Jeb said, "and Uncle Jeptha will be stringing chicken on a hook when he comes."

When night came Jeb could not sleep. The moon was gone and cold winds crawled down the high slopes and shook the limbs of the sycamore. Jeb peered from the window but he could not see the box. He thought about Grandma Quildy saying something had told her the doodlebugs were in his room. He wondered if it could have been something she had seen in the print of the Book. He wondered if the Book had the great powers she spoke of. His Uncle Jeptha always made it home from the hills. There was a chance the prayers Grandma Quildy said for him had something to do with guiding him. Jeb knew that if he lost the doodlebugs he lost the pup. If there was any chance at all, it was worth it, and so Jeb knelt beside his bed.

"Lord," he said, "I don't rightly know if it was you who told about the doodlebugs being in the room or not. I wouldn't be caring if there was a moon tonight, and I could see to the woodpile. You must know, I reckon, that they are out there; Grandma Quildy says you know everything. What I'm trying to ask is that you help me watch the doodlebugs until Uncle Jeptha comes. I can watch them myself during the day, and if you can keep an eye on them at nights for me I would be obliged. In case you don't know everything like Grandma Quildy says, I want to tell you that I think the danger is in that rooster of Grandma Quildy's. It knows the doodlebugs are there. No matter how hard I try, I can't see to the woodpile tonight. Amen."

Jeb was at the woodpile when daylight broke. In front, lying on the ground, was the box. The black dirt was scattered over the red clay of the yard, and the doodlebugs were gone. There were chicken tracks in the dirt. Jeb looked around the yard. The big domi-necker rooster stood flapping his wings beside the house. Jeb wished that pup was real and was here right now to chase that old rooster clean out of the valley. He grabbed a stick and ran after him. The rooster squawked and Grandma Quildy came out of the house.

"What are you doing to that rooster, Jeb?" Grandma Quildy called.

"It got my doodlebugs," Jeb said. "It watched me put them on the woodpile and waited until I was asleep. You knew if I was to put them there the rooster would get them! You never wanted me to have the hound pup!"

"Lord help me if I knew the rooster would get the doodlebugs," Grandma Quildy said, wringing her hands.

"Lord didn't help me last night when I asked Him to watch them," Jeb said.

"The good Lord had nothing to do with the doodle-bugs, Jeb," she said.

"He had nothing to do with guiding Uncle Jeptha home either," Jeb said. "I asked Him to help me, and He helped the rooster. It was a high climb to the woodpile and that rooster couldn't have made it himself without a light to see. Chickens are blind in the dark."

"You have no faith, Jeb," Grandma Quildy said, wiping her forehead with her apron. "If you had had, perhaps you wouldn't have needed the doodlebugs in the first place. You pretended to have faith last night, but you can't fool the Lord."

"And I don't have time to fool twelve doodlebugs," Jeb said. "How will I ever get the pup?"

"Maybe it's not too late for faith," Grandma Quildy said. "But you'd have to believe with all your heart. Last night you prayed for the Lord to watch the doodlebugs, and then you got up and went to the woodpile to see about them. You didn't have faith the Lord could watch them."

"I'll never get the pup," Jeb said.

"I'll search the print," Grandma Quildy said. "You search for faith. Wonderful things are written in that Book."

On the weekend Jeptha came. Jeb was on the hill, and it was not until he came down and saw Lucy in the yard that he knew Jeptha was there. He ran to the house.

"Did you bring the pup?" Jeb said, catching his breath.

"Bring me the doodlebugs," Jeptha said, in a slow voice. Jeb looked toward Grandma Quildy, but she only lowered her head.

"I reckon," Jeb said, "there's something I ought to tell you about the doodlebugs."

"Don't have to," Jeptha said. "Just bring them to me so I can count them."

"I don't have the doodlebugs," Jeb said. "Grandma Quildy's rooster sneaked to the woodpile where I was hiding them and ate them."

It was hard for Jeb not to cry. Yet he didn't want Jeptha to see the tears. Tears were not the mark of a man. But he had tried hard and had not shunned his work. The doodlebugs had been caught, but there was nothing Jeb had left to offer for the pup. Nothing except maybe this faith Grandma Quildy spoke about. And that seemed small compared to the box of doodlebugs. Yet it was the only chance.

"Grandma Quildy said," he said, "that faith could be counted same as doodlebugs."

"Perhaps—" Jeptha said. "Perhaps that's what it was."

Jeb looked down at Jeptha and then toward Grandma Quildy. Grandma Quildy had raised her eyes to look toward Jeptha.

"Coming through the hills this morning I had the funniest feeling," Jeptha said. "As if something was calling my name. I thought it was the wind through the trees. You know how the wind will sometimes catch in a knothole of a tree and make a sound that you can reason to be a voice. But Lucy commenced to whimper and she hung her long tail between her hind legs and hunkered close to me. I tried to make out the sound and for some reason I began to think of the doodlebugs. I thought of the work that would be left here for you to do while I was at the mill. Surely, I figured, this is only the wind and so I looked up into the tall hickories where the sound was coming from.

"I found a knothole in the tallest tree and waited for the wind to catch it again. It did, But somehow it didn't sound like the wind. I've never been as keen on faith as I ought to be, but I got sense enough to know I've been guided along the tramroads for years without asking. Maybe if I had started earlier, the trips would have been a lot shorter. Faith is a better bait than a doodlebug, Jeb, and I reckon the pup is yours."

Jeb's heart beat so loud that he was sure it could be heard across the room. Grandma Quildy laughed loud and wiped her eyes. And then Jeptha walked to the other room and came back holding the small red pup. He handed it to Jeb.

Jeb looked at the pup. It had one eye as black as the sparrows; the other eye as white as the bark of the sycamore. He looked at the broad head and long ears. And then he looked at the tail.

"Look!" he said, pointing to the stub, "Uncle Jeptha has sold the pup's tail."

"Wait a minute," Jeptha said. "How can you sell a tail when there's no tail to sell?"

"There was a tail," Jeb said. "All hound dogs have tails. There's still part of the tail left. Besides, its eyes are not even the same color. They both ought to be as black as the sparrows, like Lucy's."

"Don't you know what that white eye is for, Jeb?" Jeptha said. "That's the mark of the moon. You don't find it in one in a thousand dogs."

"I was told years ago," Jeptha continued, "by an old hunter that lived as close to the hills as the black oaks. Do you know why it is, he said, that a hound dog howls from the ridge at nights when it's got nothing treed? And why it will sit all night and bark at the moon, first on the flat, then up the slope, and then from the highest peak? Not many men would know that dog is chasing the moon. That dog is trying to find a pup. They know the moon is the sign of the night and if they can catch it, the moon will mark the pup with the signs."

"Not many dogs catch the moon. Most of the hounds give up and settle for an ordinary pup. Lucy didn't quit. She trailed night after night. And that bulldog of Chet Potter's sneaked and went with her. Sometimes I'd catch a glimpse of her along the steep ridge and hear her voice roll along the slopes. She must have climbed right up the tallest mountain and sunk her teeth into the moon. Now it's my figuring that she pulled the moon close enough to the peak for the bulldog to grab hold. The moon marked her pup with the signs of the night; a mooneye, the old hunter called it. Now, as for the tail, it was in all rights that the moon give the bulldog something if he sunk his teeth in, and I figure it was the stub tail, like the one he has. A moon-eyed hound is one in a thousand."

"Maybe we could graft a tail on the pup," Jeb said.

"The pup will be stronger with the stub," Jeptha said. "The less limbs a tree has, the more powerful the trunk. It ought to work the same on a hound dog. That's going to be a powerful pup."

"Grandma Quildy," Jeb said, "you have good eyes to see the print in the Book."

"Whatever made you think my eyes were bad?" Grandma Quildy said.

"If I were you, Jeb," Jeptha said, "I believe I'd take the pup to bed. It's small and needs lots of rest."

"Come on, Subtail," Jeb said, picking the pup up in his arms. Lucy followed behind whimpering and wagging her long tail.

Jeb tucked the covers over the pup and placed its head on the pillow beside his. Lucy curled up at the foot. The pup whimpered.

"There's no need to be afraid," Jeb said as he rubbed the pup's hair. "What you hear is only the wind in the sycamore." He looked out toward the sycamore. Then he looked up the steep slope toward the ridge. He could see the moon.

14.
Ely's Bass

HIS name was Ely, and he was a mender of fences. This was the trade he claimed to know the best, and he was willing to bargain with it for the right to fish for an old fish he called Joner. The day Pa bought the farm we inherited Ely, according to its prior owner, Tom Lucas. But before the summer was over we knew that Tom Lucas had been wrong. It had been Ely who inherited us.

It was a rough land that Pa bought. The surface lay hidden beneath scrub oak, bull thistle, and saw brier. Shaped like a bowl, the land tapered quickly from the house on the point, ending in a slice of hollow, cupping a small pond shaded by dropping willows. I saw nothing good about the land. But then, Pa always had a way of seeing things through his eyes that I could not see. His was a breed of stubborn people, a people that had learned to mold the steep ridges to fit the plow, fighting the hill country until the red clay earth nourished green seas of grass and, favored by a reasonable amount of rain, corn that often grew to more than six feet in height. He saw the second and third growth timber fall before the blades of a bulldozer and instead of scrub oak, cattle dotting the slopes fat and lazy in the sun.

The day Pa had stood on the point looking over the land with Tom Lucas I had let my eyes wander down the tall steep walls of earth to where, deep in the hollow, the small pond lay. The wind played with the willows, bending them to brush the surface.

"Good water supply for the cattle," Tom Lucas said, pointing toward the pond. "Spring-fed." A grin came to his face, and he rubbed his chin. "Good fishing, too, if you've a mind to wet a line. The fish go with the land—that is, except for Ely's bass."

Pa rubbed his chin and stared at Tom Lucas. "Ely's bass?" he asked.

"Big bass," Tom Lucas said, measuring the air with his hand, pulling them farther and farther apart.

Pa watched Tom Luca's hands closely. Pa was not a fisherman, but so wide a measurement widened his eyes. "And Ely?" Pa asked.

"Reckon I can only say what Bill Tarp said to me when I bought the land from him thinking I could make a go of it. Buy the farm, and you inherit Ely."

Pa was never a man to question. He had his land. Nothing else mattered at the moment.

The first week that we had moved to the farm a strange thing happened. It was in the evening and I had walked a distance out the ridge to where a bulldozer had pushed a stand of scrub oak into a ravine.

My job was to cut the limbs from the bigger oaks and stack the trunks so that the sun and wind could season them for winter heating. I had pulled a sizable oak from the heap when I heard a sound from farther out the ridge. I squinted my eyes and stared. But the bulldozer had not reached the distance of the sound and I could not see through the underbrush. The sound died along the slopes and I went back to trimming the oak. And then the sound came again. It was a low thud such as a man might make by beating against the side of a post and now and then there was a twang of metal. I bit the ax into the oak and crept out the ridge as quiet as if I were stalking a squirrel.

I had gone less than fifty yards when I saw him. He was an old man. Stoop-backed and his white hair blowing in the evening wind, he was mending a portion of the fence that a rotted limb from a giant oak had broken. He bent now to his knees, placed his hammer inside a small wooden box, picked up the box and a long fishing rod and turned down the slopes toward the pond. He stopped at the edge of the pond and brushed the low-hanging willows aside, stopped and fumbled inside the box. And when he raised his hand and flipped out over the water, I saw the ripples spread from the center and edge toward the bank.

During the next few days I did not mention the old man to Pa. I had little chance to. Pa was out of the house early in the mornings working alongside a bulldozer operator that he had hired to clear the land, and he seldom returned until darkness had crept over the valley. He had little time for talking. And handling the chores around the house, such as feeding the stock and getting the wood seasoned for winter, kept me busy. At least I told myself this was the reason. But actually I had a greedy motive for keeping the doings of the old man secret. Being by myself most of the time made the land a lonely place, and trying to figure out the old man with the white hair took away a great deal of the loneliness.

I soon learned his habits as far as the farm and pond were concerned. He came over the knoll each morning at daybreak and fished until the sun came up. During the heat of the day he walked the fence line, stopping here and there to strengthen a strand that had been weakened by time and weather. He returned to the pond toward evening and remained until dark. And as I crouched to watch the old man fish the pond I remembered again the words of Tom Lucas: to buy the farm is to inherit Ely. Was this Ely? It had to be.

I thought about the old man so much that I could not sleep. And so one morning I sneaked to the pond to wait for him. I watched daylight crawl down the slopes and saw the old man burst through the mist that rose from the pond and kneel beside it. I watched him take a lure from the box and tie it to the end of his line. Then he sneaked to the edge of the water as quiet as the mist and sailed the plug out across the water. It landed near the bank less than ten feet from where I crouched. He reeled slowly, squinted and saw me. He pulled his line from the water and walked to where I squatted. With one hand on his hip he stared at me and said nothing. The wind played with his white hair and his heavy eyebrows shaded eyes that seemed to be staring through me. And still he did not speak. I took a deep breath and said:

"Are—are you Ely?"

"I am," he said, and then jerked to stare at a splash in the water from the far bank. He studied the ripples closely, then looked at me again. "Tom Lucas' kin?"

"No," I said.

He rubbed his chin. "Friends visiting, maybe?" he asked.

"No," I said. "My name is Bob Anders. My Pa bought this farm from Mr. Lucas."

"Eh!" he grunted. "Tom Lucas sell out?"

"Yes," I said.

The old man walked to where he had laid his wooden box and picked it up. He took the plug from the end of the line and turned up the slope.

"It's all right," I hollered after the old man. "Pa will let you fish here."

He turned and stared at me. "Young man, I ain't a man to take privileges without earning them!" And he walked farther up the slope.

"But Pa don't care if you catch the big bass," I hollered.

He turned quickly. "What bass?" he asked.

"The big bass," I said, moving my hands as far apart as they would go. And seeing the old man frown his eyes, and thinking maybe the short length of my arms had caused me to do injustice to the fish, I added: "And then some."

A grin came to the corner of his mouth and disappeared quickly.

"Your pa home?" he asked.

"Yes," I answered.

He turned up the slope toward the house.

"Can I come with you?" I asked.

"Young man," he answered, "I am the trespasser."

Pa stood in the front yard stretching his arms into the morning air, shuffling his feet, uneasy, waiting for the bulldozer operator to report to work. He turned his head quickly as the old man walked into the yard. The old man wasted no time. He stopped in front of Pa, set his fishing gear on the ground and placed his hands on his hips and sized Pa up. "Knowed Tom Lucas wouldn't last," he grumbled. "Tell he was a lowland farmer the day I seen him. Know'd the hills would whup him." He looked Pa over again. Then he stretched out his hand. "Ely Tate," he said. "I've come to bargain."

"George Anders," Pa said, seeming still off balance under the stare of the old man. Yet I thought I caught a slight grin on Pa's face. "What are you bargaining for?" Pa asked.

"A fish," the old man said.

"A fish?" Pa rubbed his chin.

The old man stood silent, a frown on his face. I thought he might be disgusted that Pa had not heard of the great fish and so to save Pa embarrassment I stood behind the old man and stretched my hands apart to measure the fish, hoping to remind Pa of the day Tom Lucas had spoken of it. And when no expression came from Pa's face I said, "And then some!"

"Oh yes," Pa said, rubbing his chin. "I believe I heard Tom Lucas say something about a big bass that was the granddaddy of the pond."

"I come to bargain for him," Ely said.

"Well," Pa said, "I see no reason why you can't just go right on fishing for him."

Ely scratched his head and frowned his face in disgust. "Let me tell you something, young man," he said. "You just don't take a fish like old Joner over there without earning him!"

"Well," Pa said, "I'm not much of a fisherman, but if you been after that fish as long as Tom Lucas said you have, I'd say to catch him would be earning enough."

"What's between me and that fish, is between just me and that fish," the old man said. "I've come to bargain."

"Then what is your bargain?" Pa asked.

"I'd like to work for the right to fish the pond," the old man said, "until the fish is caught."

"What kind of work?" Pa asked. "Im not a man to tell another what he can best do."

"Well," the old man said. "Mr. Tarp, he owned the place before Tom Lucas, judged me to be good at mending fences. Tom Lucas found me decent at the same."

"It's an honest trade," Pa said. "And it would be most welcome around here." And they sealed the bargain with a shake of the hand.

The old man picked up his gear and started out the

ridge. I followed him for a ways hoping that he would turn again toward the pond. Bur farther out he stopped and grinned. "Old Joner is through feeding for the day. He feeds of the mornings and of the evenings, sprawls out in the cool of the pond when the sun is high." The grin left his face and he frowned at me. "You'd best start earning your keep here at the farm. Your pa needs your help. The land is rough." And seeing the frown come to my face, he softened his own. "And then some," he said, and his laugh drifted behind him through the underbrush.

Each morning now after my chores I sat under the willows at the pond and waited for the old man. Each morning he came down the path, opened the wooden box and tied a plug on his line. The wooden box was full of lures, and he had carved them all himself. They looked so real that each time he opened the box I expected them to jump out and start running through the weeds. Each morning he started at one end, walking and casting until he had circled the pond. Some mornings after a cast I would watch the line zip through the water and the rod bend. The old man would brace himself, his eyes growing wide. But after a few turns of the reel the smile would leave his face, and he would bring the smaller fish to the bank.

I hated to see the sun come over the ridge. Morning became short, and day began to seem longer. During the heat of the day I thought of the old man and sometimes I got to worrying that maybe the sun wouldn't set or that he might grow tired of fishing for the great bass and leave. But always, just when I was feeling the lowest, I would cock my ear to the sound that came from along the fence line somewhere out the ridge, and I knew that the old man would be watching the sun and still earning the right to fish the pond.

One evening he told me more about the great bass. "It was an evening about like this," he said. "The line didn't zip like when some of the smaller fish take it. It just sorta eased out into the pond. I thought it might be a small bass that had hold of a plug bigger than his mouth would let him swallow. I was fishing with the best plug I had ever made. It was a plug that had took enough years of thinking to gray my hair. And enough casting for the right weight to stretch a line over the moon. And enough fine carving to bring callouses the size of acorns. I gave the line a twitch, just a little twitch. It felt like I had hooked a steer.

"I reckon I fought that fish all over the pond, giving and taking line. And then he stopped. There was more fight to him just gliding through the water than there is to most fish. I knew when I looked at him here at the edge of the pond that he was worth all my years of whittling and then some. Biggest bass I ever seen. What I didn't know was that he was playing possum. I reached for him, thinking how I would carry him home, mount him over the fireplace and just sit and look at him. My hand touched the water and the next thing I knew I was blinded by spray. By the time my eyes cleared old Joner leaped high out of the water from the center of the pond allowing me one last look at my plug. Just seemed to have a big grin on his face. I 'lowed then and there that one day I'd take that fish, and take him right."

There were times as summer was ending that I did not get to go to the pond. Pa had brought more cattle to the farm, and I traveled with him each day to neighboring farms to buy hay to winter them. It would be the second year before we had a stand of grass on the red clay solid enough to cut. Most times we would get home before dark, and I would run to the fence and look toward the pond. And I would see the old man walking the slope to the ridge. I squinted my eyes hoping he would be carrying nothing besides his fishing gear. It was not that I didn't want the old man to catch the fish; I just wanted to be there when he did.

Autumn came and the brown leaves sailed through the air like meadowlarks and lit on the small blades of the first stand of grass on the slopes. Pa stood at the fence, his foot propped on a board. He was staring toward the pond.

"You know, Bob," he said, "it takes a lot of work and planning to make a good farm."

I looked out over the land and for the first time I think I saw what Pa had seen the first day he had stood beside the fence. Much of the land was now cleared, and open to the sun and rain.

"Sometimes there are things you have to do that might not seem right at first," he said. "Things that have got to be done if you are to have a good farm." He rubbed his chin. I looked at him, not understanding. "Bob," he said, "I want you to listen close to what I have to say. After all, one day this land will belong to you, And what we do now will determine how good the land will be."

I looked at Pa. He was staring over the slope toward the hollow. "It's about the pond," he said. "The pond must be moved."

I stared toward the pond without saying a word.

"Before you say anything," he said, "I want you to hear me out. I want you to know that I, too, have thought of Ely and the big fish, Joner. I know that the old man has worked hard for the fish. I've never had to go back on a bargain before."

"But how can he catch the bass," I asked, "if the pond isn't there?"

"I said the pond must be moved," Pa said, "not destroyed. It was bad judgment to put it where it is in the first place. The pond covers good land. It should have been built farther down the hollow, letting the water spread over the rocks where the land is practically useless for crops. There it would have served its purpose as a water supply. And it would hold the water much better than it does here."

"Can we wait until winter comes?" I said. "Maybe Ely will catch the bass by then."

"The land will be frozen too hard to work then," Pa said. "It must be done now. We'll build a dam below and allow the water from the upper pond to run down into it. Judging from the size of the level pipe through the clay dam, I would say that most all the fish can ride through it into the new pond."

"What about old Joner?" I said.

Pa frowned his face. "I'll try to settle with the old man for the work he's done."

I sat under the willows waiting for Ely to come down the slope. The sun had gone from above the ridge and I knew that darkness would come early now that autumn was here. For the first time I did not feel happy when I saw the old man coming.

He moved quickly around the pond to where I sat, a grin on his face. He knelt beside me and opened the wooden box.

"Look, Bob," he said, holding a new plug. "Old Joner is in for it now." He stared at me and squinted his eyes. "Well, now what's the matter? Don't you think it favors a bluegill minnow? Dogged if your eyes ain't become almost as particular as old Joner's. But it'll look better in the water."

I said, "Pa's going to move the pond." I said it flat out.

The old man stared. He did not speak, and I watched him place the new plug back inside the box.

"He's going to move it down the hollow into the trees and rocks," I said, pointing with my finger.

"I reckon I knowed it," he said at last. "Reckon I knowed it all the time. Knowed it the day I saw him. There is a difference in your pa and the others that owned the land. The pond is in the wrong place, and I knew that the eyes of a good farmer would catch it. Reckon I was hoping that it might take him a little longer. Even a little time is precious to an old man."

"What can we do?" I said, frowning.

He set his lips. "Wipe the frowns from our faces

first of all," he said. "It would shame a great fish such as old Joner to think there was two quitters trying to outfox him."

I set my lips, trying to look as stubborn as Ely.

"That's more like it," he said. "Now let's bargain."

Pa must have suspected the old man would be coming once he got word of the pond. He was standing in the yard as if he were waiting. He stretched out his hand as the old man walked up.

"I guess," Pa said, "you wouldn't consider pay for the work you've done?"

"Reckon I wouldn't," Ely said, scratching his head. "But there might be another way."

"Name it," Pa said.

"When you drain the pond most of the smaller fish can get through the pipe. But not old Joner. And if a man was to wait beside the pond until the water was low enough to show his fins, he might step in the water and grab him. I've come to bargain for that right."

Dad stretched out his hand. "The fish is yours."

"Shucks, Mr. Anders, you just don't take a fish like old Joner without working for him."

A smile came to Pa's face.

"All right," he said. "What is it you want to do?"

"Help drain the pond and build the other dam," the old man said.

The dam was built lower in the trees, the old man working in the dust behind the bulldozer. And after the lower dam was built the valve was opened on the upper dam. Ely stood beside the pond watching the water gush through the pipe. The pond waters eased through the pipe and he kept a watchful eye. Here and there smaller fish jumped, and then, caught in the current, were sucked through the pipe. Everything was going along just as we had planned for it to go.

And then it happened. From the edge of the pond there came a great spash and a large fish leaped high into the air. He leaped again and again and each time he fell back into the water there was less of it to cover him until at last he landed in the soft mud and could not wiggle loose. Ely splashed through the water and muck and stood over him, his eyes wide. He straddled him, ran his fingers through his gills and pulled the fish from the water.

"Reckon," he said, looking at Pa, "I'm obliged to you."

He turned up the slope, carrying the huge fish and stopping now and then to look back to where the new pond filled deeper in the hollow. I could see his lips move as if he were talking to the fish but I couldn't hear him. The old man was leaving for good. No more mending fences. There was nothing more to earn. I rubbed my eyes and stared after him. I squinted. Something was wrong. He was coming back. And then I felt Pa's hand on my shoulder.

"I'll be doggone," he said, "I'll be doggone."

The old man walked past us to the edge of the new pond. Here he knelt and looked at the great bass. He held the fish so close to the water that his tail splashed in it. And then he moved his hand out and the next thing I knew the old bass was breaking water from the center of the new pond. Ely got to his feet and walked toward us.

"That weren't no way to take a fish like Joner," he said. And he walked away.

Pa shook his head. "Sure hate to see the old fellow go. Best fence mender I ever saw."

The sun was still above the ridge as we went toward the house. But the day was growing late. As I walked through the field I thought of the old man and my eyes watered. I rubbed scoot under the fence. But then eyes watered. I rubbed them to keep Pa from seeing and started to scoot under the fence. But then I stopped. Pa stopped too. He stared at me and a smile as large as the one he had the first day he looked over his land came to his face. From out the ridge there drifted a sound. It was such as a man might make if he were pounding against the side of a post. Pa looked down at me. His expression made me feel good all over.

"Feel like bargaining, son?" he said. "You're part owner of the land, you know."

I grinned back at Pa. "I could use a good fence mender," I said. And I stood beside the fence waiting for the old man to come to strike his bargain for the right to fish the new pond, a bargain that was sure to include me as a partner.

15.

The Culture of a Hounddog

IT was one of them things that you never expect to happen but does and leaves you sitting around wondering if it really did when you know it did. And then trying to figure if you had handled it different it might have turned out all right. A thing you can't blame a fellow for not believing. And I'm not holding you to believe it. But it *did* happen, and I'm still siting here trying to figure it ou tand can't.

I mean look at it from my side. It was just like you'd expect, me and that dog. You know, man's best friend and all that. A big old rawboned bluetick whose name was Drummer until I had to change it toward the end. A tail that was too long for him, legs bowed more than they ought, one ear shorter than the other, and a liking for running a cold trail which was a fault. A little less than a normal hound with a voice that wouldn't be apt to bring a brag.

But we tolerated each other and might have made it if we hadn't moved to the last house in the hollow over on Carr Creek. And, even then, we made it for a while. I mean he'd stretch out during the day scratching fleas like a hound dog has always got and has to scratch. And now and then I'd pick up my fiddle and strike out on either *Arkansaw Traveler* or *Billy in the Lowground* or *Fire on the Mountain*. He liked music, even back then, though I paid it no attention to amount to anything. And mostly after dark we'd take a traipse into the hills and try to strike up a possum trail or two, hot or cold. It didn't make any difference to that hound. Like I say, he'd take a cold trail, which was a fault. But he was company, and I figured I probably had faults too.

But then warm weather came, and cars started coming up the hollow, and since they couldn't go no farther they pulled up down from our house and stopped. Young couples up the hollow to spark and all that. Motor running and radios blaring and I always have said this younger generation is all hard of hearing. I mean the music from the radio was loud enough to shake the walls of the house, which old Drummer seemed to like and I tolerated. But it was when they got ready to drive back out of the hollow that was really something. I mean they had no place to turn the car around and no intentions of backing. They tore up the yard, got stuck, tore up the fence, figured to sit another hour, and then raced the engine until it sounded like a swarm of bees about ready to bust their wings. I don't see how it kept from blowing up.

Well, it got so bad that one day I figured I ought to do something about it. I said, Drummer, let's me and you hook up the mule and drag out a turning place down there at the end of the road before they back up and tear the house down.

It was a mistake. I mean dragging out a turning place. Instead of taking it to be a turning ground, they took it for a parking lot, told their friends and they moved in. So now instead of one couple up there at nights, it got to be three and four. And they raced their motors like they were sending out codes to one another and every radio played a different station, which Drummer liked but which bothered me because they never played my kind of music. I mean it was that jumpy stuff that won't make a go around here and has nothing for me to catch on the fiddle even if I wanted.

But, even with all the ruckus, me and Drummer still managed to keep our schedule. Well, most of it. We went out on the warm nights all right to traipse the woods and strike up a possum, but when we headed home we started stopping on top of the knoll over-looking the parking lot. I'd do some staring till I got a crook in my neck and Drummer would listen to the music and lift his nose into the air now and then and let out a mournful bawl. Well, you can't blame me or the hound for that. I mean it was little payment for the work we had done and the noise we had tolerated. And it did make me feel some younger and helped my gout. It didn't seem to bring any harm. I mean how was I to know that when old Drummer stuck his nose into the air he was trying to sing? He just looked like an ordinary hound to me. So I didn't take any stock

when his deep voice began to change and get a hig screech to it.

Then one night, with my neck crooked and sore from the night before, I decided not to go. Drummer went without me. Along toward midnight his screeching and yelping got so bad that I figured someone must have backed over him or something and so I walked over. Poor Drummer, I thought. But when I got there, there he was sitting on the knoll, the radios blaring and him trying to imitate the lot of them. And doing a right decent job. I mean now and then I could make out that he was carrying the tune and when he popped to his all fours and cracked a *C* in the end of his tail I said, Uh oh, something is up. I mean old Drummer always carried his tail between his legs and here it was curled up over his back now, trembling and shaking and making all kinds of little forms that reminded me of notes like you find in a songbook.

Good grief, I thought, could it be that this ain't no ordinary hound? This hound could be gifted. But, he's after the wrong music. I mean, like I said, jumpy stuff just won't go around here. But if he could be toned down to country music and a man could slip him down to Nashville, he could stand back and watch out for the gravy. I mean who ever heard of such a thing: a singing hound. My days of chasing possums is over, I thought. I'll be rich.

So I started getting my fiddle out during the day more often and playing a little to him while he stretched out there by the fire. But all he done was twitch around uneasy, cover his ears with his paw and live only till dark when he could get back to the parking lot. Time seemed to be running out on me. But if I could just get this hound to take up what would go here in the hills, he could support me. And so when he left at night to go over to the knoll I started setting about to find out more about music. I got me some books in Sourwood and read what I could of them and it all began to fit. I mean his sounds and the curling of his tail. The way I saw it, that hound had practiced until he was able to get up to a high *C*; that accounted for the curl I had seen that night in his tail. Not only was he singing, but he was shaping the notes as he went along. I better sweeten up to this hound, I thought.

But he kept getting more and more independent until at last I decided to change his name from Drummer. I called him Highbrow, which I thought was fitting seeing his highfalutin new ways. He seemed to like it. At least he would look my way when I called him by it. And I started doing all sorts of little things that I thought would show him that it was me and him through thick and thin. In other words, if I couldn't beat that dog, I aimed to join him.

And then something came over me. I mean I got the feeling that this hound was trying to cut me out. Little things that he done. I lost sleep worrying about it and come up with a fever and then worried more because I got to thinking he might sneak off and leave me while I was weak in my joints. Now when he sneaked over to the knoll at nights, as sick as I was, I crept through the bushes to keep an eye on him. My fever got worse in the night air and I even worried some about all the things that might be going on down there in the parking lot and me not able to see.

This hound is going places, I said. If I just nurse this fever and keep him from getting away, a sack won't hold the money I'll make as his agent. But I kept getting weaker and weaker, just knowing the hound was turning against me.

I got so sick with worrying and staying up late at nights that I overslept one morning and when I woke up old Highbrow was gone.

Well, I was too weak to travel to look for him. I had to settle for inquiring. I traced him down the Kentucky side of the river to where he had crossed into Cincinnati. Someone said that he got himself hooked up with some sort of conservatory school of music over there. From Cincinnati he went to Boston and joined an outfit called the Boston Pups or something like that. Far as I know he's still in Boston.

Well, they may have got him all right. But I'll tell them people up there something: he'll cold-trail a possum every time. And once he gets all musicked up, he'll leave them, too. He'll cut out for Nashville; they always do.

16.

A Sack Full of Faith

THE boy sat on the banks of the river under the shade of the low-hanging willow limbs watching the wind blow the white cotton blooms of the willows onto th esurface of the water. The blooms fell so light that the ripples that came from them could not stretch to touch the edge of the bank. The blooms drifted with the lazy current, hugged the shoreline, and curved like long white ribbons downriver.

To the boy the river and the willows were the most wonderful of all things. Perhaps this was because he could walk along the bank and there would be no one to stare or point a finger at him. In town, where he lived, they did. Or he imagined they did. He felt them staring at his long hair which reached his shoulders and was matted like the nest of the catbird that chose the willows for its home. Or, if it were not his hair, then it was the many patches his mother had sewed on his clothes. He did not like to stay long in town, and always hurried from it to the river and the willow grove. There was no fingers or eyes on the river or among the willows to point or see and laugh.

On the bank of the river he would sit and wipe tears from his eyes as he felt his long hair. He could not understand why it was made to grow if it was wrong in doing so.

He did not think his hair being long was nearly as bad as mother's red hands; red from washing clothes over a rough board until they were clean for other poeple to wear. It was a means she must use to earn money, and she had told him that one day when she had washed enough clothes she would have his hair cut by an honest-to-goodness barber like other boys and let his hair remain short.

To the boy, there looked to be enough water in the river to wash all the dirt from the face of the earth. And along the sandy banks grew enough willows to sift the hottest sun and spread shade deep into the sand to cool his feet. You did not have to wash clothes over a rough board to pay for it. All it cost was the walk down the bank.

One day he asked his mother where the beautiful river and the willows came from and she told him they had been made by God, the same as everything else. But the boy had no knowledge of God and he was confused. There was only one thing he knew: anyone who could make a river as pretty as this and sprinkle the willows along it had to be great. And so he thought now of God. And he thought of his long hair and patched clothes and his right to be on the river. One day he had asked his mother where God lived and she had pointed her finger toward the steep mountain in back of the river and said that God lived above the clouds that circled it.

"But how could you ever get there to thank Him for something?" the boy had asked.

"You don't need to go there," his mother had replied. "He can hear you just as well under the willows you are always talking about. God will seek you out."

The boy still did not understand. And during the days that followed, he sat along the river staring at the clouds above the mountain. And he thought that he didn't even know what God looked like. He tried to shape God's face in the clouds that gathered and trailed off across the sky. And he wondered if God would get mad because he tried to shape Him with long hair and patched clothes. He thought there should be a place on earth where he could go and thank God. And so he said to his mother:

"Does God stay above the clouds all the time? Won't He ever come down?"

His mother looked up from the tub of clothes she was scrubbing. She squeezed suds from her red hands and brushed her hair out of her eyes.

"There's a church near the mouth of the river," she said. "I have heard He comes there."

"Can you see Him?" the boy asked.

"Can you see the wind in the trees? his mother asked.

"But how can you know for sure He's there if you can't see Him?" the boy asked.

"How do you know the wind is among the willows?" she said.

"I can feel it," the boy answered.

"There is no difference between the wind and God," she said.

"Do people go to the church to thank Him?" the boy asked.

"Some do," she answered.

The boy watched her rub her hands. The skin was broken in places and the strong lye soap had swelled the open flesh and he knew that it stung. And he felt sorry for his mother. He had asked to help her many times, but she had always said that he was too little just yet, that now was his time for play, while he was too young to know troubles.

"Have you ever been to the church to thank Him?" the boy asked.

"Yes," his mother said. "A long time ago when your father was living."

His mother was busy again washing clothes and she did not talk anymore.

On Sundays the boy began to sneak to the mouth of the river, hide in the willow grove that grew to the top of the riverbank, and stare at the people as they went in and out of the church. And as he watched, a frown came to his face. They had no patches on their clothes, and the boys all had short hair.

His long hair and patched clothes worried him more now. He wondered if only people who had no patches or long hair were allowed inside the curch. But he was ashamed to ask his mother. Maybe, he thought, the church is for people who have patchless clothes and also have money to have their hair cut; maybe the river and the willows are for boys like myself. If this were so, he thought, God has surely cheated those people.

But soon he knew different. The boys who went inside the church also came on the hot days to sit under the willows along the river. And the boy began to think. If these boys could sit under the shade of the willows and stick their feet into the cool river, then why couldn't he walk inside the church also? He felt his hair and he knew the reason. He remembered his mother's words. He could thank God for all he had under the willows as well. The river and the willows could be his church.

Winter came to the river and the leaves fell from the trees and the river rose and carried them away. The wrinkled bark of the trees was exposed to the sun, naked and lonely-looking. But the wind was cool and there was no need for shade. The boy thought the river was still very beautiful. To take the place of the cotton blooms and leaves the winter brought layers of ice to the edge of the river, captured leaves inside the ice and the meager sun turned the great border of ice and leaves into a million colors.

Christmas would soon be in the valley and this day the boy had gone to the mouth of the river, following the border of ice, picking out all of the different forms of the leaves. He heard some boys coming down the bank and he hid behind the trunk of an old and warped sycamore tree. The boys were talking about sacks of candy that all the young people would be given at the church the coming Sunday. All one had to do was walk up and get it. He watched the boys scoop up stones and trhow them on the ice, listening to the thin ice crack, and watching the thin lines of the break eat out along the ice like the unraveling of a fishing line. Watching the splinters of ice, the boy thought of the candy and of the money it would cost —more money than he would probably ever have.

In the days that followed he thought only of the sack of candy. He looked over the river, silent with winter, and imagined a path across it that he would walk to the church. He would snatch the sack of candy and hurry back to the river. If he was fast, people could not stare long. And the stares might be worth a sack of candy.

As Christmas Day drew nearer he began to sneak closer to the church and measure the distance between the riverbank and the church. And the more he measured the greater the distance seemed to become. He thought of something else: once he was inside the church he would not have time to thank God for the river and the willows and the candy. But, then, he reasoned that he could make up for it when he got back to the river.

On Christmas morning the boy left the house early. He was nervous and he did not want his mother to notice this. He had kept the thoughts of the sack of candy to himself and now he would keep the plan to go into the church for it to himself. Then he would not have to tell his mother if he failed.

He went to the mouth of the river and waited until

everyone was inside the church. His plan was to take a deep breath and make his way to the church as fast as possible, so he would not have time to think and maybe change his mind. And so he ran and did not stop until he was at the church door. He stood silently for a moment, glancing back toward the river. He swallowed and looked at the door. He tried to imagine the door being like an opening to the river. Trembling, he opened the door and stepped inside.

At the far end of the room he saw a table, and a woman standing behind it. On the table were sacks of what he thought had to be candy. The table was a long ways from the door. The woman called out something and a group of girls stood up from the row of benches. They passed down the aisle as names were called, one by one. Each took a sack of candy and returned to where she sat. Next, a group of boys stood up and went and got their candy. And then another. The boy waited until the boys he had seen at the river stood up. His heart beat fast, for he had not planned anything like this. He had thought that all he had to do was go inside the church, pick up a sack of the candy, and go back to the river. To have to go with a group frightened and confused him, but it was too late to turn back. He fell in at the end of the line of boys moving toward the table, keeping his eyes on the floor.

When he reached the table the woman spoke.

"What class are you in, young man?" she asked.

"I don't believe he belongs here," another woman standing behind the first one said, "but give him some candy anyway."

Tears sprang to the boy's eyes and for a moment

he was too frightened to move. He turned and all he could see were eyes staring—staring. He lost all sense of being. He knew only that he must get back to the river—to the willows. The candy was not his to take. He turned and ran up the aisle. And he did not stop until he was back by the river, under the willows.

After a while he heard a sound from the willows on the bank above him. He looked up to see an old man standing in the riverbank, his long white hair blowing in the winter wind. Behind the old man was a group of boys, the very boys that the boy had so often watched come to the river during the hot summer days.

The old man held a white sack in his hand and the boys fidgeted and shuffled their shoes in the sand.

"I am Reverend Sanders," the old man said. "The boys and I want you to have this." And he handed the boy the sack of candy.

The boy took the sack, and, because he was ashamed, he lowered his head. But through the corners of his eyes he could still see the old man. The old man was scanning the sky and the land around him. He breathed deep of the river air.

"God's world is beautiful," he said. He motioned to the boys. "We will give thanks here on His river."

The old man knelt in the sand and the boys gathered around him. And the boy joined them, and as he did so, he thought of his mother. She had been right: God had sought him out.

17.

Fur in the Hickory

"YOU can talk about that new repeating rifle of yours all you want," the old man said to the boy as they made their way up the slope of the hill toward the ridge where the shagbark hickories grew. "It's your gun and only natural that you ought to have some feeling for it. But me? When I go for squirrel I aim to put meat on the table. You don't see me carrying repeating rifle, either. I take my old musket. Been with me a long time. Went through the war together. Brought a brag once from General Morgan himself." The old man stroked the barrel of the musket and jerked it into firing position. "Yep, when I lay an eye down the sights, I want to know there's fur under the hickory. It's the eye, too, Jacob. Remember that. The eye is one of the reasons you see so many fellows carrying them repeating rifles now days. Afraid one shot won't do it. Don't trust their eye or their gun. So they go to repeaters to cut down the odds."

The weeds along the path were wet from a light

rain, and the old man, walking in front, took up some of the rain with his britches legs and the pants made a low whistling noise. Daylight was beginning to break over the ridge, and no wind was stirring. The trees were taking shape. Birds were stirring in the tree limbs along the path and as they moved in the wet branches the boy cocked his ears, thinking that the noise might be a squirrel jumping through the trees, traveling to the hickories on the ridge. It was a good way to locate squirrels, listening for the sprays of water made by squirrels hitting the limbs. The old man had taught him this.

On the ridge the old man stepped ever so lightly. He stopped under a shagbark hickory. Daylight was shifting fast now through the limbs of the trees. The old man stopped and picked up a half-chewed nut. He held it close to his face.

"Sampling," he said, pushing the nut into a pocket. "Too low on the ridge yet." And he looked off to where the ridge peaked. He glanced again at the new repeating rifle the boy carried.

"Times have changed," he said, walking stoop-shouldered. "When I was a boy your age I'd have been laughed out of the mountains for carrying a gun like that. If you had to shoot more than once at the same target you went back to practicing. And squirrels! If you hit a squirrel with a bullet, you didn't dare take him home. Bark 'em, that's what we did. Hit the tree right under the squirrel's chin and knocked the wind from 'im. Not a scratch on the squirrel. Everyone carried a musket and no one hit a squirrel." The old man

leaned against the side of a black oak and took a deep breath. "Wasn't that we couldn't get a repeater, either. City fellows came around all the time trying to sell guns like the one you tote. But when you made a brag then in the hills, you had to prove it. And no man ever came that could match his gun against a musket. I ain't wanting to brag, but I never got beat."

The old man picked out a black oak on the ridge and sat down at its foot. Less than fifty feet away stood a large shagbark. The boy sat down beside him and stared at the leafless limbs of the hickory.

"If I'd a had to use a repeating rifle, I probably would've quit long ago," the old man said, placing the musket across his lap and stroking the long barrel. "They didn't call me Barkem Tilson for nothing, you know. But you got too many Sunday hunters now. Highfalutin outfits, and just move in and blow the tops out of the trees. But not me. When I shoot, there's just one ball. When I look down the barrel, there's business coming out the other end."

The light broke now and shone on the old man's long gray hair and beard. Sweat caused by the long walk up the mountain ran down the wrinkles of his face. He took a piece of homemade twist from his pocket, balled it in his hands and stuck it in his jaw.

"Can't rightly expect a fellow to do much shooting today, though, I reckon," he said. "The world's moving too fast for them. And they don't have to depend on their guns like we did. Not even in wars like they have today. I mean they get back miles away and bang away at one another. Never see the man that fired the gun. But with General Morgan you had to look the enemy in the eye. Just bring them repeating guns in here today and blow a squirrel beyond recognition. Most times don't even bother to skin it out. Just hang it on a fence somewhere and let the crows have it. Just wanted to kill it, not eat it. Want to take the spite of the whole world out on as little a thing as a squirrel. We never done that. What we killed we ate. What we couldn't eat we let grow until we got hungry again. Not many of the fellows today would carry a gun heavy as a musket. You just ask your ma. She can tell you I always kept meat on the table when she was growing up. You got to get close to your gun, Jacob. Treat it like a woman. But you're a little young yet to know about that."

The boy placed the repeating rifle across his knee, in the same position that the old man had placed the musket.

"Listen!" the old man said, just above a whisper. A light spray of rain fell and made a noise hitting the brown, autumn leaves on the ground. The spray was too even to have been caused by the wind and too heavy too have been caused by a bird. The boy looked toward the shagbark. He saw the bushy, gray tail of the squirrel blowing in the morning wind that had begun to work in the tops of the trees. The old man had the musket to his shoulder. His hands were unsteady as he tried to level the long barrel of the musket. He squinted his eye, opened it, and looked once more down the long barrel. Then the sound of the gun echoed through the woods, and a few birds took wing.

The boy watched the gray squirrel slide behind a limb and disappear. The old man lowered the musket, rubbed his eyes, and wiped the sweat from his face.

"Knocked the wind from that gray," he said. "Thought your old grandpa was just blowing to the wind, didn't you? Too old to be traipsing the mountains, your ma said. Shaw. I saw that ball nip the bark right under his chin. Go pick him up, Jacob. I'll reload. Be careful you don't scratch the barrel of that new repeating rifle of yours against one of them saplings on the way. You'd best waited for the musket to be yours." And the old man chuckled so hard that the boy saw his teeth.

The boy walked under the hickory. He stirred the dead leaves. He didn't know what he should do. He couldn't tell the old man that he had seen the squirrel slide behind a limb and then cross out. He watched the old man as he slid the rod down the musket barrel. The old man was still grinning. Finally, the boy walked back to the oak and stood in front of the old man.

"Didn't find a mark on the squirrel, did you?" the old man said, looking up and grinning.

"I couldn't find the squirrel," the boy said. "Maybe he crawled under the dead leaves on the ground and hid. Those leaves are heavy and a squirrel will do that."

"Don't I know that!" the old man said. "I taught it to you. But it didn't happen that way with this squirrel. Now if you can't see a squirrel stretched out on the ground how do you ever expect to see one in a tree? You got to use your eyes, boy."

The old man got to his feet, frown on his face. He

walked over under the shagbark, the musket swinging limp in his hand. He kicked at the leaves, scattering them over the ground in heaps. Then he put his hand on a young sapling and shook it. The boy knew that the old man was testing to see if the squirrel was still in the shagbark. If the squirrel was there the movement and noise from the sapling would cause him to move and be detected. But the boy knew no squirrel would move. The squirrel was gone. The old man had missed.

"I think I'll go on out the ridge and sit a spell," the boy said.

The old man didn't answer. He was staring into the shagbark.

The boy walked along the ridge, picked a good spot and sat down. And he thought of the old man. How sad he had looked. How he had kept his eyes off him while he looked for the squirrel. And he remembered his mother telling that he should watch after the old man. He was pretty feeble. Shouldn't be going so high on the mountain at his age. But that he would keep right on going so long as there was breath to him. The boy worried. He got up and sneaked back out the ridge to check on the old man.

He saw that the old man was back sitting beneath the oak. The musket was across his lap and his head was bent on his chest. He was asleep.

On his way back out the ridge the boy heard a spray of water hit the ground. He froze and turned his head slowly. The big gray squirrel ran along the limb of an oak and stopped in the fork of the tree. The boy raised his rifle slowly. He took a deep breath and tried to remember all that the old man had told him. He aimed under the squirrel's chin. He squeezed the trigger and the squirrel fell. The boy picked him up and looked quickly for signs of a mark. But there was no mark on the squirrel. The boy had barked his first squirrel and he felt proud and happy. He tucked the squirrel under his belt.

The old man was still under the oak with his head dropped. The boy sneaked under the shagbark and placed the squirrel in open sight. Then he sneaked away and hid behind a tree. He bent, picked up a rock and threw it under the shagbark. The old man jumped at the noise. He looked around. And then his eyes rested on the shagbark and he rose to his feet. He saw the squirrel before he was under the tree. He grinned, looked around, picked the squirrel up and examined it. Then he tucked it under his belt and walked back to the oak and sat down.

The boy waited a while longer before he walked to the oak.

"I heard a shot," the old man said. "Did you get him?"

"I thought I had him, Grandpa," the boy said. "But I must have shot just as he jumped."

The old man rose again to his feet. The bushy tail of the big gray stuck from his belt. The boy looked at the squirrel.

"I didn't hear you shoot again, Grandpa," he said.

"Didn't shoot again," the old man said, grinning.

"Then you found the squirrel under the shagbark!" the boy said.

"Found him?" the old man said. "Never was lost. Right there under the tree all the time. Just wanted to see if you had learned to use your eyes. Well, don't worry. You got a long way to go, but you'll make a hunter."

The old man scanned the tops of the trees. The wind was heavy now. The woods were noisy.

"Wind's too strong to hunt more now," the old man said. "Maybe I'll give you the chance to try that repeating gun of yours again in the morning. Or maybe you'll be wanting to borrow my musket."

The old man laughted as he walked down the ridge and the musket swung back and forth in his arms.

"I'd like that, Grandpa," the boy said.

18.
Of Greed and Eb Ringtom

WHENEVER I think about how greediness once got hold of me, I want to crawl off in a hole somewhere and die. I mean you got no way of knowing how terrible and powerful it is unless you've tangled with it once and been cleaned out yourself. Then life ain't worth living.

I was standing in high clover. I had all of two greenback dollars—and plans for spending them that took a backseat to nothing. I mean if you had seen Tallie Marcum down at the Baptist Revival that Sunday, the way she big-eyed me during the singing of Canaan Land. Girls what look like Tallie don't have to go around picking on strays.

Well, she big-eyed me on Sunday and I started cutting at a cord of wood for Sam Bascum on Monday. Sam runs the feed store down at the mouth of Bear Creek and sells everything from aspirins to horse collars. He'd pay on Saturday and I'd be back down there on Sunday at revival with some green to back me up. I had plans to ask Tallie Marcum if she'd maybe like to take in a movie on Monday night. Try to get acquainted ahead of the other boys since Tallie had just moved in down where Tom Ramey used to live and was new here. From where she lived it couldn't of been no more than a three-mile walking distance to the movie house. I figured if she'd be willing to walk we could get by on a dollar, including a little popcorn during the main feature, and some to eat on the way home. You know, do it up right, first class. Then I'd still have this big green I'd be saving, and if me and Tallie worked up all right I'd have something to make another turn with. Not like blowing it all in one shot and having nothing left to reload with.

I got the cord of wood finished for Sam around five o'clock on Saturday, which didn't leave me much time being that I wanted to make a sashay around Tallie Marcum's house to see if any of the fellows were hanging around down there. So I hurried into the feed store and said:

"All done there, Sam."

He counted out the two dollars, and I turned to go out the door. That's when I saw Eb Ringtom sitting over in one corner of a feed sack forking his finger for me to come closer. Well, Eb is one fellow I don't know too much about except that he lives close by. For Eb it was a small shack stuck on the side of a hill up a spur hollow off Bear Creek called Roe Branch. You seen him now and then grubbing along the hills for other people—saw briers, scrub timber, and black-berry vines—him looking old and weathered under a hot sun but not supposed to tire from it. Somehow you never expected to see a man like Eb doing anything else, just like he was part of the land and meant to do just that. And then you could, and expected to, see him on the road any Saturday going to or coming from the feed store with a brown coffee sack slung over his shoulder to carry a week's grub in. Fact is, I couldn't picture him without his old broad-rimmed hat on his head to ward off the sun and a sack over his back. The rest of him was sort of quiet and mysterious as a shadow.

I scooted a little closer to Eb but still kept my sights on the door knowing that time was running out and if the boys were hanging around down there at Tallie's house they'd be able to hide in the bushes on me after dark.

He looked at me, then off, his eyes searching the store like there might be someone else there besides me and Sam. And he said:

"How'd you like to double that money?"

I guess it was then that greediness set root, but I sure didn't figure so at the time. I just sorta looked at Sam Bascum like saying what's coming off here and Sam grinned and winked at me. This must have been the point that greediness broke ground because I never took Sam's grin and wink to mean anything except he was steering me in on a sure thing.

Well, I never seen much luck before, just always went around knowing that sooner or later it could come my way. So I said:

"How do you mean?"

I could see right off that this Eb Ringtom wasn't a man to slip one in on you. I could tell by the way he kept his voice low and made sure there was no one around close enough to hear. That's the way I figured luck would come slipping in. I mean luck just don't come calling to everyone; it singles you out.

Eb looked at me like I'm being auctioned off and he said:

"Maybe you wouldn't be the sort that would want to double that money at all."

Well, like I say, there it was. Luck no more than four foot from me.

Eb looked at Sam Bascum and said:

"What you think, Sam?"

"Well, he done a good job on that cord of wood."

And Eb, he takes another look around to keep luck from being a Santa Claus and he says:

"Be over at my place at seven o'clock."

Well, I didn't know if I could do that. I didn't like to shuck luck off and say no right then. But on the other hand to be there I'd have to give up my sashay around Tallie Marcum's place. And if the fellows were down there, seen her, and she as much as blinked an eye, they's bird-dog that place until daylight.

Besides I was in pretty good shape as it stood. I had money to sport. I could walk in at revival maybe letting a little of that green stick out of my pocket, enough to show but not fall out and get lost. Maybe pin it inside my pocket and leave half of it out. She ought to go for the reckless type.

Eb just picked up his grab sack and walked out the door, winked and said:

"It's your lucky day, boy."

I tried to fight it off. But the more I thought about that two dollars growing to four the weaker I got. I mean I was lapping at greed like a thirsty dog. Why, with four dollars I could have that looker throwing rocks at the other fellows. I could pin a green from each pocket and set her eyes in her head. A dollar each trip to the movie house comes to four times, after which I could probably be as independent as a grasshopper in a summer cornfield. I mean even lookers don't go around giving up a man of means. And I could stretch it all out until Sam Bascum got low on wood again.

Well, I shuffled with greed up Roe Branch at seven o'clock and found Eb sitting there on the porch with a big rawboned hound stretched out at his feet. He glanced down at my pocket and saw the green sticking out there that I had pinned to let him know I had come to face up to luck.

"Careful a brier don't snatch that money from you," he said, "before it gets a chance to grow twice its size. Well, you watch old Thusla here and see that he don't get into the woods, and I'll get ready to go. That hound turns his mind to possums when the moon starts out."

I stood guard, the big old dog scratching, while Eb walked through the shadows and into a shed near the rear of his shack. The minute Eb had turned his back the big dog had started to snore. But I didn't figure him to be a part of luck anyway. "I could be wrong," he says, "but somehow you look like the sort to me what could take a little responsibility." He struggled with the rooster. "I could let you take old Thusla. Nope. You're all right. I'm going to let you carry this rooster."

He shoved the rooster into my arms, Thusla growled

and caused that rooster to ruffle and raise a welt on my arm with his sharp bill.

"Know what you're holding there?" Eb asked.

"Chicken, ain't it?" I answered.

Eb twitched his mouth to one side and says:

"I see you don't know nothing about gamecock fighting. Better take another look."

I didn't know a thing about gamecock fighting except what I caught from the Parson now and then down at church and it was all bad, gamecock fighting that is. But figuring luck wasn't going to put up much with my ignorance I took another look at that chicken determined to see something else.

"He's a gamecock, ain't he?" I said.

"He's more than that," Eb said. "He's a champion. The best in these hills. Napoleon the Champion, they call him. "Bring on the roosters, bring on the wildcats, bydogged bring on what you got and I'll match old Napoleon against it!"

The big rooster ruffled again and raised a welt this time just above my srist.

Well, I looked at that chicken now with pure intentions of showing a little respect. He was taking on the look of luck.

"He's a pretty thing," I said.

Eb stretched back and looked at me like a man of some means.

"You're sure lucky," he said. "I've turned a lot of fellows away from what you got coming free tonight. I mean that Napoleon don't even bring your sweat. Don't go shuffling and pecking and showing off down there with that other rooster. Goes in the pit and gets the job done." He gave a little, low growling laugh like you do sometimes when you got the other fellow dead-to-center, and I growled back, only greedier.

"I'm mighty grateful," I said.

"We'll just take our time going up the hollow to Ben Willard's barn," Eb said. "Give them suckers up there enough time to get their betting spirits up a little and go to betting crazy. You wouldn't get a penny put up against old Napoleon otherwise." He pointed his crooked finger at me. "You ought to be ashamed, boy, taking their money that way." But he was grinning from ear to ear.

And I went up that hollow carrying that rooster and feeling sorry for no one. I mean feathered luck in my hand, Thusla under my feet, and Tallie Marcum everywhere I looked. It was the other fellow's tough luck. I had waited long enough on luck.

Thusla worried me the most. I could feel my pocket easy enough to make sure a brier didn't pick me clean, but that big hound was tripping me every other step of the way causing Napoleon to ruffle and raise more welts on me. Me getting a break only when Eb stopped to catch his breath. Then old Thusla would edge over close to Eb, stick his nose to the ground and sniff like a fool.

"Look at that hound!" Eb would say. "What that dog can't sniff out ain't worth talking about."

"But don't he ever get into the woods any?" I asked, wanting relief since I didn't know how much longer my tired legs could outstep him.

"If he was an ordinary dog he might," Eb said. "But he ain't. No Thusla. If a possum sneaks across the path, he's going to have the strength to run it. He don't go lagging his strength off up there in the bushes."

The rest of the way I didn't have just Thusla to worry about because I had got to worrying about not being able to find anyone there at the barn to strike a bet with me. I mean two dollars in one wad might arouse suspicion. I was plain miserable.

Well, I'd have enough to choose from. That barn was packed with people, most of them gathered around a pit built with green-oak timber. Two roosters shuffled inside it. A few men looked at Eb when we walked in; some grinned, some laughed and one said out loud:

"Old Eb's brought the champion again."

Then they all laughed, which made me feel both good and bad. Good because I was certain now that old Napoleon was a sure thing, and bad because he'd let everyone in the place know about the champion, and I'd be lucky to strike a bet.

Eb, he just looks as many as he can in the eye, me figuring he's gauging to see who the sucker is that's about ready to fatten my pocket. Then he breaks away and I see him talking to a man over in one corner of the barn, and I ease up just in case any green has got to show. The big rooster, he keeps trying to break free, with me knowing if he gets down he'll probably show his stuff, attack some rooster outright before I can get my money on him. I had my hands full.

Well, I could see right off I wasn't going to get no bets from this fellow. He was a sorry-looking sight. The sort you can look at and see he ain't nothing but a common loafter and not apt to have a penny to rattle. Just standing there like a tramp with sawdust all over him which told you he had been wallowing on the floor, and an old pair of glasses on with both lens cracked and spidered.

"Well, there's the champion," he said, me walking up and liking him all the less for them words. For several people turned to laugh again, this time at the little feller I hoped. Then I can see him squinting at the rooster. "I don't believe I'd let that boy carry the champion with his head hung down," he says.

And Eb looks at the rooster and then back at the man and says:

"Cletis, you're a fool!"

"Set him down and let's take a better look," Cletis says. "Let's see the old champion stand."

Eb nodded and I set the rooster on the sawdust, holding his wings so he couldn't attack. Cletis, he moves back a little and bug-eyes the chicken.

"I never seen the likes, Eb," he said. "Right up there on the tip of his bill. You ain't aiming to fight that rooster with him on his head, are you?"

"Just you clear the way, you old fool," Eb said. "If you've had time to bum that many drinks things ought to be right for betting."

He picked up Napoleon and I followed him toward the pit. He looked down at me, cupped his mouth and whispered at me, "Get your money down."

And I looked over the crowd trying to see how I'd like to help me escort luck in. I shucked up to a big fellow who was looking at Eb and that rooster like he might not know either and I said:

"Wouldn't want to put down about two dollars against that rooster, would you?"

He looked me right in the eye.

"You wouldn't be kidding would you?" he said.

I thought maybe he wanted to see the green being that it was a pretty good hunk to be hit with, so I peeled it out before his eyes. Sure hoped he wouldn't ask for odds.

"You're covered," he said, just a little faster than I thought he ought. He reached down and picked them greens from me and says: "Ain't no use your getting attached to 'em any longer than need be; only makes it all the harder to see 'em fly away."

And Cletis, he comes up about now and whispers:

"You don't want to lay that good money down on that chicken. Forget that there rooster and let's me and you get us a jug."

I don't pay no attention to Cletis. I'm staying close to this big fellow that's got my greens. It was the first time I had been away from them. I kept one eye on Eb. He was inside the pit now, and old Napoleon was facing a big, black rooster. And everyone was grinning and watching Eb and Napoleon. Well, it wouldn't be long before I'd have my greens back. I mean I was lonesome without them.

I tell you it happened so fast. I mean that big, black rooster shuffled and pecked and headed right at old Napoleon. Couldn't have reached him, the way I seen it, but old Napoleon just flops over on his back and pops his legs into the air like he's set out on the table for eating. I thought I seen him pop one eye open to see if the other rooster was laying off. Course, I could have been wrong, being as how my eyes were misty about now. I mean shucks almighty I got my greens on that chicken. Then I hears Cletis. He says:

"I knew that rooster was a goner standing on his head like that."

And the next think I knew Eb was carrying that rooster toward the door with the saddest look on his face. I trailed along behind trying to clear my head and think what's happened to me.

Outside the door Eb handed me the rooster. Eb's all puckered up and tears are coming from his eyes.

"Hold the old champion," he said, his voice all broken and wobbly.

I took one look at the coward of a chicken and I said:

"If he had only just shuffled. I mean if he had only made an effort to fight instead of just flopping over flat on his back like that. Shucks, that ain't much of a way for a man't life earnings to be snuffed out!"

Eb sniffles and says:

"He went out like a real champion. Just got plumb tired of killing. They go that way, champions do. Just give up the ghost giving some poor chicken a break."

"But my greens," I said. "I been wiped out clean."

"A trifling," Eb said. "Don't little that rooster with talk of it. You paid a small fee for witnessing the end of a champion."

Well, life was over for me. I knew it. It was doubtful if I could start again. Me holding a dead rooster up here in the head of a hollow and the rest of the fellows down there big-eying Tallie Marcum. Me standing here a pauper fixing to shed myself of this chicken.

"Well," I said, "what do you want to do with this chicken?"

"What rightly ought to be done with a champion," Eb said. "We'll bury old Napoleon. Lay him to rest peaceful-like."

And while Eb took another drink I looked down at the rooster and again I thought I seen him pop one eye open. But it could have been rigor mortis, or something like that.

I could see that Eb was plenty sorrowful and I figured I'd have to play the game out and help the best I could. Burying him wouldn't be too bad. The ground was still warm and soft and over there under some hollow beeches it wouldn't take long to scoop out a hole and be more than the rooster deserved.

I walked over, stared scooping out a little hole, and Eb looks at me and says:

"What are you doing there?"

"I'm burying this rooster," I said, "and all I got in this world, or had, along with him."

"Now ain't you ashamed," Eb said, puckering his mouth again. "Ain't you ashamed to insult the old champion and him a short time above ground."

Well, this sorta took me back for a minute, so I took another look at the rooster. Nope, I was ashamed of nothing about a rooster that's died of fright.

"What do you mean?" I asked.

A quarter of a mile on down the hollow I found out. Eb turned and pointed his crooked finger toward the sky and said:

"There's only one place to lay old Napoleon. The burial grounds of the champions. On top of Sourwood Mountain where he'll be overlooking the valley."

Sourwood Mountain! I mean if you stretched out flat of your back on a bright day you couldn't see the top of it. The slopes of it raw and naked except for saw briers, sourwood sprouts, and cold, gray rocks laying thick like the land had been warted by a frog. A long, long way to bury a chicken. A coward at that.

"All that way to bury a chicken!" I said.

"Hold your tongue, you ungrateful sort!" Eb said. "It's a champion you got there.Pick up his head a little so that it won't hang down so much and hold him high to the grave." And that Thusla dog looked at me in the worst way now that I was down and out. And me breaking path for that critter over miles of rough country! He was backing Eb up to the hilt.

So up the slope we went. Up where it got lighter since we were getting closer to the sky. Eb in front, and me still breaking path for Thusla and carrying that chicken, so tired I could hardly stand up.

When I reached the top Eb was sitting there still looking sorrowful. I took hold of the rim and pulled me, Thusla and the rooster over. Funny thing that that rooster was still limp as a dishcloth. Never got stiff. And the top of the mountain wasn't a thing but little scooped-out holes. I looked at Eb and said:

"My, my! If someone ain't been doing a lot of digging up here!"

"Not just diggins, boy," Eb said. "Them's all the holes of champions. Just sunk in a little from the weather. Get you a stick and dig in about that point over there. It'll let the old champion rest a little ahead of the others. He'd like that."

Well, I got me a stob and scooted out the best I could. The earth was as tough as a rock. Eb, he sits all this time with the tears running down his face.

"I'm calling back the times me and the old champion has seen together," he said. "I'm glad you're here to dig his resting place and cover him over. I wouldn't have the heart to do it."

I dug until I thought I'd pass out and then I placed the rooster in the hole and started to cover him over. And there was no mistake about it: that rooster opened one eye. He blinked it a few times and then settled it on that handful of dirt I was holding.

"Eb!" I said.

"I know it's hard to cover him," Eb said. "But you got to do it. You ain't nearly as close to that rooster as me. Close your eyes and push it in."

"Eb!" I said. "This rooster has blinked his eye at me. There, he's done it again!"

"Hold your wicked tongue!" Eb snorted. "I could take that like you're meaning I been harboring a coward Ain't there no respect in you?"

Eb stumbled over toward the hole and squatted. There was a ruffling of feathers and Eb fell back out of the way. Out of the hole came the rooster, squawking and running toward the rim of the mountain. He took wing and sailed over the top, clearing the sourwood sprouts and all.

"Great balls of fire!" Eb said. "Old Napoleon has up and flew to the Great Beyond. Who'd ever believe it. Mountain just wasn't tall enough to hold the likes of him!" He turned and swarped Thusla across the nose and said, "Get your nose out of my britches leg and face the wind, you coward!"

We made our way down the side of the mountain. And near the foot of it we passed a small shack of a farmhouse, one end against the hill and the other on stilts. Eb, he stops just long enough to say to an old man sitting there on the porch:

"Ain't seen the likes of a rooster what's flying high, have you?"

The fellow looks out and says:

"Saw old Napoleon, Eb. Just sailing on into the Great Beyond. Just about that cloud there to your right."

Eb shakes his head like that's really something and stumbles on. And me, I get to thinking about that fellow sitting there knowing the name and all of that rooster and where he's supposed to be heading. Me knowing that the rooster is just up ahead of us since I can hear him in the brush. I said:

"You know old Napoleon?"

"Know him!" the man said. "You can set your watch by that rooster running past here on fight nights up in the hollow. Old Eb has got the top of that mountain dug up like a plowed field. Got someone new with him to do the digging every time he goes up. Sure hope you never done no fool betting on that Napoleon rooster like all the others."

And there I was. Took in by greed. My two dollars shucked down to the size of a little hole in the ground and me wishing I could crawl in it and die.